Chapter 1

Sophie pushed the freshly painted shutters o[
warm air flooded into the coolness of the room. The welcoming
warmth of the early spring sunrays kissed her cheeks. Her eyes
widened at the perfectly framed elevated view before her. Her
vision feasted on the endless horizon, dramatic white cliffs
studded with lush green pine forests and the various shades of the
sea below that could keep an artist busy for a lifetime. Sophie
never tired of seeing the panoramic vista of colours the tiny island
of Ithaca fed her soul. She still had to pinch herself to believe that
she was actually living in this Greek paradise and this beautiful
house that would soon be called home. Closing her eyes, Sophie
breathed in the heady scent of the rosemary as the fresh spring
breeze stirred the gentle fragrance from the gardens surrounding
the house. The aroma reminded her so much of Nikolas. Nikolas,
she thought as it sent a broad smile across her face and a quiver of
excitement through her body.

Spinning herself around, she looked into the welcoming calmness
of the stylish room that she had spent the past few months
creating. It was now so different from when she had first visited
all those months previous. The sad neglect and unwelcoming
emptiness was now a distant memory as she sympathetically
added the final touches that made it feel more like a home again,
without removing every trace of its previous occupant. She hadn't
wanted to erase Evangeline's memory entirely. Not just at that
moment. There would be plenty of time for her to put her own
stamp on it.

Sophie had spent almost all of her free time at the house through
spring after the weather had turned more pleasant. She had
finally built up enough confidence to brave driving the mountain
roads alone. Erika had accompanied her in the car on her maiden
Greek driving experience, just to give her Dutch courage. It had
been great to have her witty company at the house and her
knowledge in identifying the abundance of native plants in the

1

gardens was exceptionally useful, as this had been an area that Sophie was not that confident to tackle herself. But most of her time had been spent alone in the companionship of just the Greek radio presenters that she could not understand regardless of the Greek lessons from Erika through winter. But, a few retro tunes she could dance to and sing along with, had blurted out from the dated radio that sat on the kitchen windowsill making her time in the house not feel so isolating.

Days of laboriously sanding down the years of flaking paint from all the woodwork had completely ruined her nails and left blisters on her fingertips. Her shoulders and neck had ached for weeks after she had washed down all the interior and exterior walls before giving everything a fresh coat of white emulsion making it gleam in the returning sun. Her back and legs had been in agony after clearing away the overgrowth around the tiers of rosemary in the garden, trimming and trailing the unruly grape vine on the pagoda and from giving the place a good general clean removing years of dust and cobwebs from every crevice. It was amazing what a lick of fresh paint actually did to replace the sadness of its past and inject life back into such a pretty yet forlorn home. It was now almost ready for their new start when Nikolas eventually arrived back from Athens.

That day had seemed such a long time away, she thought, as her mind rewound to the start of winter. Those long cold months had loomed ahead of her as Nikolas had left for the mainland early October. But finally, after months of being apart, Nikolas was due home for the start of the new tourist season and arriving that afternoon with his daughter, Maria. Sophie was determined to make the place look so homely as it would be Maria's first visit to where she had been born. She had been adamant with Nikolas that her nursery was untouched and that Evangeline's belongings had remained on the bedroom dressing table for Maria to see, protecting her mother's memory fiercely. This, Nikolas had found admirable, as he would have understood if Sophie had wanted his late wife's memory removed from her future home.

Naively, Sophie had thought that the time without Nikolas would fly by and she could busy herself along with Erika as company. How wrong could she have been? Those weeks apart were harder than she had ever imagined. She had never considered how isolating and difficult life on the island would have been. There had been no shopping malls to pass the time, gyms for her to join just to shed the extra pounds or takeaways to devour after a Friday or Saturday night out clubbing. Life here had been almost non-existent in the early weeks and had sometimes brought Sophie to the brink of returning to the UK until the following spring when Nikolas had returned. With stormy seas stopping his monthly visits and limited flights to the neighbouring island, she had not seen Nikolas as much as they had hoped. Instead, she had spent many nights sobbing her frustration and loneliness down the phone to him and wishing winter over.

Yet, over the winter months, she had learnt so many customs and traditions of the Ithacan ways from Erika and the villagers in Kioni. She had been made to feel very welcome by many of the locals joining in with their card games and coffee mornings. She had mastered a few traditional dishes under the constant watch and tuition of Erika, ready to impress Nikolas when they moved to their own home on his return. Sophie had also learnt how to speak some basic Greek. It was just enough to get by at the local shops and to converse a little with the villagers, but it had gained her a little respect for her efforts. She had also attended church a few times with Erika, who had pointed out that this was such an essential part of their culture. She had explained that if she were to be welcomed into the hearts of her fellow neighbours, going to church would give her the golden key.

Kioni had been a beautiful place to be through late summer and last of the busy tourist season. With lots of boats still arriving packed with visitors, the dock was a constant hive of activity. Large groups of people swarmed the narrow back streets and dusty donkey tracks, clicking away frantically with their cameras, eager to capture the passionate Ithacan way of life that this little village community had retained. They had filled the restaurants with their excited chatter as they shared a delicious meal whilst in complete awe of this picturesque little village port. Live music had played in the tavernas through the pleasant September evenings reaching Erika's house across the bay. They had sat out on the veranda sipping wine in the warmth of the evening breeze, surrounded by the heady scent of jasmine, sage and thyme, enjoying the music and atmosphere under the brightness of the stars so visible from the lack of light pollution.

During the end of the summer season, Nikolas had taken Sophie back to Agia Efimia on the island of Kefalonia for a visit to the Sea Rock Taverna where another spontaneous night of dancing and never ending shots of Tequila had given her another hangover from hell. They had stayed at Nikolas' rented house above the neighbouring village of Sami for a few days allowing them some quality time alone, revisiting Melissani caves. Here, Nikolas had told her of the lover's tradition of lowering their joined hands into the magical waters, blessing them with eternal love. Sophie had experienced her first small Earthquake tremor having been woken up in the early hours, by the loud bangs of the window shutter rattling against the windowpane. She had woken Nikolas in fright thinking that there had been someone trying to get in. But, having realised that the lampshade above was swinging and the bed trembling by itself for a change, he had reassured her that this was just a mild one and nothing to panic over.

They had many days out in Evangeline exploring around more of the coastline of Ithaca. Nikolas pointed out his best friend, Andreas, Yoga retreat that was perfectly hidden away in the hills above the millionaires mile of Aghios Ioannis, overlooking the calming emeralds and aqua of the Ionian sea towards Kephalonia. They had made love on the pure white pebbles of many empty hidden coves, under the light of the stars wrapped in each other's arms, as the warm waters had lapped their naked bodies. Nikolas had surprised her with countless candlelit dinners on the deck of his boat while moored around the shores of neighbouring uninhabited islands with the occasional school of dolphins joining them on their adventures. Their time together had made them

4

almost inseparable, with Nikolas surprising her gifts and flowers almost daily. He explained that as he would be away for many months, these gifts were to remind Sophie of how she made his heart sing again.

Erika had chuckled as she mocked playfully, "Beware of a Greek man bearing gifts, he may want more than you are willing to give or he wants to go to the taverna with the other men alone!"

As autumn had slowly crept in, Nikolas had returned his boat to Sami for winter storage, and they had spent more time exploring the coastline around Kioni on foot. By the end of September, the nights were beginning to get chillier and the visitor numbers had started to dwindle as the boat excursions had slowed. Only a few hardy sailors had docked their sailing yachts in the harbour to buy provisions or eat meals in the now quieter tavernas. As October arrived, almost all the tourist shops and tavernas had packed away their outdoor tables, pulled their shutters closed, leaving Kioni harbour in complete darkness. With the lack of footfall, all that could now be heard was the lapping of the waves and clinks of the sailing boat masts in the sea breeze that were docked in the safety of the bay.

Stefano, Anna and their children had arrived at Erika's in time for Marida. This was an annual festival that took place on Polis Bay in the north of the island. It signified the end of summer and the return of the fishing season. The pungent smell of freshly caught fish being fried filled the air with a heady salty aroma of the sea as a large crowd had gathered from all over the island. Everyone who had attended, feasted on a banquet of fried sardines, a vibrant rainbow of Greek salad and freshly baked bread blessed by a local priest.

Sophie sat wrapped in a cardigan, keeping her warm from the chill of the approaching dusk, watching the setting sun over the open vistas of the horizon with Nikolas' arms wrapped around her waist. She absorbed in wonder, the many stories told to her about Ithaca and its culture as she glowed under the ambience of candlelight as darkness had arrived. Sophie hadn't laughed so much in a long time. She had met so many new friends who had fallen in love with the island during a holiday and moved their lives from the UK to live out their retirement in paradise. Exchanging their contact details, they encouraged her to join their regular meets as they all supported each other while away from loved ones. She had drunken copious amounts of Ouzo and red wine making Sophie a little tipsy.

A group of ladies in traditional costume had performed Greek folk dancing while a group sang and played mandolins. Even though he knew her co-ordination was terrible, Sophie had been dragged reluctantly from her seat by Nikolas to join in the dancing. He had laughed uncontrollably as Sophie stumbled her way through the dance. She continually tripped over her own feet and trod on those of the dancers next to her, as she tried hard to get the rhythm of the dance. Feeling slightly embarrassed by her lack of co-ordination, Sophie had been glad to return to her chair and hide in amongst the crowds.

Clusters of children fished or took a night time swim in the still-warm waters, while their parents, and grandparents, enjoyed time with their friends. The atmosphere had been electric and jovial as those with summer businesses had let their hair down and enjoyed a moment of relaxation for the first time in months. It had been an incredible experience for Sophie, and she had returned to Erika's that night filled with so much more love for the welcoming inhabitants of this incredibly humble island she was just discovering.

Nikolas had left a few days after the festival, heading for his winter work in Athens, leaving Sophie heartbroken in his absence. Then, as if someone had turned on a tap, the rains came. It had rained continually for days, creating muddy floods that had rushed down the empty streets taking anything moveable with its fast and furious flow and eventually spewing it into the sea below. This had kept Sophie and Erika prisoners in the house for days on end to avoid being washed into the increasingly stormy seas. They had spent the time baking, listening to the radio and Erika's favourite past time, card poker.

Erika had shared beautiful memories of her childhood on Kefalonia and later on Ithaca with her young family. She had explained that the streetlights were relatively new on Ithaca, having only arrived when Nikolas had been a young boy. Before this they had wandered the village in the complete darkness of the night and her husband often fell into the sea after a late night at the local taverna's. Regardless of the heavy rainfall, Erika had explained that clean water had once been so scarce in Kioni that water pirates would deliver it by boat, selling it to the villagers to drink. Sophie had laughed with the tales of her first time getting drunk at the age of just five when she had helped her Uncle treading grapes in a square concrete vat called a Lino. After watching the juice, trickle into the podohi where it was collected, she had helped to pour it into the clean barrels. Here it was left to ferment for exactly sixty-five days, Erika had sneakily drunk far too much of the potent juice thinking it was just fruit juice, making her feel very tipsy.

Sophie was left holding her aching stomach from laughing so much at Erika's tales of her Yiayia's reaction when TV finally arrived on the islands. How she couldn't understand how the people got inside without a staircase. Erika had been told to change from her nightwear into her best dress, so she looked nice for the small people on television and to keep her legs closed so they could not see up her skirt. Sophie had almost wet herself laughing when Erika informed her when cars arrived on the island, the locals had tried to feed them hay as they had no idea what to do with the metal version of their beloved donkey or horse. These were stories that the villagers held dear to their hearts and shared with anyone who had time to listen. Time with Erika was definitely not dull as she had so many stories to entertain Sophie through the long winter nights.

Philoxenia had escaped any severe flooding that winter, but a few of the houses on the other side of the bay had not been so lucky.

As Kioni was built on a steep hillside, the rainwater would regularly rush through the network of trees above bringing devastation for those in its path. Erika had told her of times that she had been forced to remain on the upper floor of the house. Muddy water had flooded the ground level caused by a landslide from the newly developed land above her. Those were the worst times when Nikolas had to come and rescued her to take her to the safety of his house high in the mountains in Exoghi. Those were the times when the church bells would toll almost weekly as they lost yet another neighbour to the storms in Kioni.

Sophie had braved the local shop during short lulls in the weather a few times to buy necessities, but with no boats visiting due to the tempestuous behaviour of the sea, the shop's stocks were also running low. This meant a white-knuckle drive as passenger next to a short sighted Erika all the way to Vathy to shop at the more substantial food stores. Erika could hardly see over the steering wheel and after so many near misses with a herd of mountain goats and numerous wrong turns down a farmers track, they had eventually arrived unscathed.

Nikolas and his daughter Maria had managed to catch a flight from Athens to Kefalonia, and then, after a few days' delay due to storms, they had caught the ferry from Sami to Ithaca to spend their first Christmas with Sophie. Christmas had been a very different affair that year to what she would have typically experienced. The traditions were so far from what she had known all her life. There were no drunken nights out partying or clubbing until dawn, nor spending hundreds of pounds on pointless gifts that no one really wanted. No tacky Christmas jumpers, Queens's speech or drunken uncles to contend with. This Christmas had taught her the values of the Greek way of life.

The Ithacan's on the island followed a Greek Orthodox religion, so celebrated the religious calendar devoutly, which Sophie found so fascinating. The only time she had ever followed a religion was a short stint at Sunday school at her local church that had lasted for a few weeks. During her pre-teens, she had begged her mother to attend after she had developed a crush on one of the older choirboys. After he had rejected her flirting attempts for another chorister, a string of rebel boyfriends had arrived into her life. This had meant that she would not even consider spending her Sundays at church as it was seen as so uncool.

As December had arrived, Erika had started her fasting and busied herself decorating the house with evergreen branches, wild red berries and myrtle. She had placed shallow wooden bowls of water where sprigs of basil, entwined around a cross, were dangled from a wire. Erika would ritually sprinkle the waters around each room every morning to keep the Killantzaroi away. She explained to Sophie that these were very small wicked demons, part animal part human, that would wreak havoc in the home if they had gained access had she not been prepared, destroying and devouring everything in sight. The log fire had to also be kept alight for twelve days and nights of Epiphany to stop these demons from sneaking down the chimney.

The house had also become very busy with Stefano, Anna and their three children now staying in the compact dwelling. They had arrived the night before Christmas Eve and created a little bit of chaos to the usual serenity and calmness of the family home. Everyone was uprooted to accommodate the new arrivals. Maria had moved out of the smallest room and taken her belongings into Erika's bedroom to share her bed. Nikolas and Sophie had left the larger guest room and made do with the smallest bedroom, sharing a slightly larger than single bed. Stefano and Anna shared the double bed in the guest room, topping and tailing with their daughter with both boys on blow-up mattresses on the bedroom floor. Most mornings, Sophie would discover Stefano fast asleep on the settee finding solace from a night of little rest. Breakfast had also become like a military operation as they all woke and filled into the kitchen at different times with Erika adamant that she would make everyone's food no matter how long it took.

Yet the children had filled the house with so much energy and excitement for the upcoming celebrations. Sophie had not seen

Erika smile so much. Her man friend Felipe had joined them for an evening of food and drink on a few occasions but gracefully declined an invitation to stay over, making light tracks home as quickly as possible before Erika could convince him otherwise. The sweet scent of caramelised sugar wafted through the house as the children had helped bake traditional honey cakes and almond cookies with Maria.

While Erika had taught Sophie how to bake Christopsomo, a traditional bread made to eat on Christmas Eve. Erika had decorated with a cross and cut out dough fish, symbolising their family trade. She had sprinkled it with ground walnuts and almonds to help bring another productive year to their home, and as Erika had hoped out loudly, maybe a new baby, nudging Sophie with her arm and making her blush. This was when Erika was at her happiest. Her home filled with her family's laughter. The smell of her cooking constantly filled the air with mouth-watering fragrances of herbs, spices, and sugary sweetness as a riot of cooking was now underway in preparation for the numerous feasts ahead.

Stefano had spent the day of Christmas Eve building a small wooden boat with his eldest son, Demetrius, and decorated it with lanterns with the other two children, Xander and Selena. Then, placed it bow inwards at the front door as the children searched everywhere for anything golden that they could find to fill it in honour of Saint Nicholas, the patron saint of sailors. There was a token potted Christmas tree in the corner of the room with sweet treats and lights hung from its branches and a nativity scene lit by small candles to its base. Outside, tree trunks had been wrapped in fairy lights in the gardens that ascended the hill bringing light to the darkness of the mountains that loomed above. The villagers had lit up everything surrounding their homes including the few fishing boats left in harbour that had been illuminated with string lights which sparkled on the water, creating twinkles from their reflections across the bay. The whole scene was the most humble, yet, most beautiful that Sophie had ever witnessed.

Chapter 2

On Christmas Eve, the carol singing had started. Local children stood proudly at the door banging drums and metal triangles, singing their hearts out in return for a handful of sweets that Erika gave them after listening to their whole performance with her hands clasping her heart and saying, "You all sing like angels, my home will be so blessed for next year. Thank you, thank you little ones." Erika explained that these carols were known as Kalanta, a form of blessing for the family. Later into the day, they had all descended to the village, accompanied by their neighbours holding guitars and mandolins, singing the regional Kalanta carols. Then, their hearts filled with smiles and joy, they had retreated from the cold to be greeted by the warmth of Philoxenia.

Taking a seat in the overcrowded living room, Sophie watched as simple contentment seemed to ooze out of everyone. Stefano had thrown olive wood, vine and Schinus, a type of red-berried shrub, onto the fire for good fortune, making the room smell divine. Erika had returned to the living room with the Christopsomo, an additional circle of bread she had baked, and a bowl of olive oil and a bottle of wine. Nikolas, being the oldest man of the house, had shared the Christopsomo amongst them all. Then they had each taken turns dipping their piece into the wine and oil, then throwing it through the bread circle and into the fire whilst they all sang a traditional hymn by candlelit.

This had been the most atmospheric Christmas Sophie had ever known steeped in traditions that were worlds apart from her family ones at home. There was no dreaded game of Monopoly that lasted for an eternity, no tin of Roses chocolates to delve into or regular Christmas repeat of Die Hard with Bruce Willis to watch yet again on the television as Mum prepared the turkey and Dad snored in the armchair spilling his whiskey over himself as he slept. There had been no Coca Cola adverts and constant commercials with reminders that the 'Big Guy in red" was coming.

Christmas day had also been a unique experience for Sophie as she had come downstairs to just a small cluster of gifts by the fireplace, only receiving a small gift each. Erika had explained that their tradition was to receive their main presents on New Years' day from Saint Vasilis and not Santa like the rest of the world. The children loved receiving gifts on both days as Anna had continued to celebrate it in her own traditional ways bringing the best of both worlds to the family. Nikolas had bought Sophie a beautiful necklace handcrafted to his own unique design by the skilled jeweller located in Kioni village. No one had ever taken the time to design anything for her before. Nikolas confided that he had spent many nights in Athens, creating the necklace to be just perfect to portray her beautiful heart.

Christmas lunch was not the traditional roast she had expected, but a spread of seasonal salad, a variety of starters and a thick goat soup with eggs and lemon as Erika had been keen to uphold traditions of the past. After a glug of homemade wine, Sophie could hardly move for the remainder of the day, even when the many neighbours came to visit with more food offerings and drinks.

There had been a much-needed lull between Christmas and New Year, but the eating had not stopped with Erika creating so many delicious meals for her family and baking the traditional and very moreish Ithacan sweet Rizo-Rovani. This had been the most sensational eating experience for Sophie as she had only eaten dessert rice in her Mothers homemade creamy pudding, but this little slice of sweetness was like heaven on her palate. With its heady aroma of cloves, cinnamon and nutmeg and a sticky toffee-like crust that sent a syrup of delight through her taste buds, it made a second or third slice irresistible. Sophie had noticed the weight that she was starting to pile onto her already over-sized hips and potbelly as Erika's cooking was always so delicious and very self-indulgent as she didn't go for fat-free or lighter versions.

Nikolas and Sophie had managed to hide away at their Exoghi home to enjoy a little calmness and spend some much needed intimate time together. They had removed most of the old furniture and taken it to a family friend who owned a repair shop and ordered new from a furniture shop in Vathy. Nikolas had packed a picnic, which they had eaten on the living room floor of the once abandoned house, with the log fire roaring, keeping them both warm from the winter chill. Nikolas had played his guitar and sung his Greek love songs to her in his raspy voice that had melted Sophie's heart. With candles lighting up an atmospheric glow across the room, they had made love in front of the leaping flames of the fire in the complete silence of the night.

Everything with Nikolas felt so perfect and Sophie often felt like she was in one of her 1950s Hollywood movies. How had this gentle caring man ended up in her life at the most perfect time? How time had changed since her days of existence with James back in the UK and the unrealistic pressure she had placed on herself to be happy. Here she didn't have to try to be anything. Living on Ithaca had calmed her desire to battle with her childhood expectations of true happiness. Just being with Nikolas was enough for her. The urgent desire for marriage and children had long diminished as she had now found so much peace and pure love.

Through Epiphany, Sophie learnt so much about the importance of the ancient, almost Pagan traditions and the superstitions that the islanders believed in. It allowed them to celebrate their lives with daily optimism and gave them so much hope for their future. This way of living felt very peaceful to Sophie. She no longer felt insulted when the older ladies pretended to spit three times, muttering "na min avaskathis", as she walked by after Erika explained this was to protect her from the evil eye and was not in distaste as she had first thought. Even though she knew it was meant as protection, Sophie still couldn't get used to them actually showering her in spit by mistake, as she was wiped down her face or dress for the umpteenth time.

On New Year's Eve, they had all gone for a walk with a spade in hand in search of a plant called Kremyda. This took them out of the village and across the rocks following the coast towards the derelict windmills. The walk was pleasant, and even though the sea air was now becoming chillier by the day, they had chatted, explored the ruins and laughed for most of the walk until they found what they were after growing in abundance from between the rocky crevices. Uprooting one of the plants, they headed back to the warmth of the house where Erika hung it, roots and all, on the door to ward off evil spirits and bring them all good luck.

During the final evening of the year, they had met all the locals in the village by the church, danced, drank and ate more to celebrate the coming year. As the New Year was banged in, they had sprinkled each other with perfume and cologne before heading back to their beds with warm hearts, cold noses and all smelling like the fragrance counter in Debenhams.

New Years Day had been another day of excitement. The children had received their presents from Saint Vasilis, eaten honey-soaked pancakes for breakfast and set to work helping Erika bake Vasilopita, a cake that she hid a coin inside, much like Christmas pudding tradition back at home. They had eaten Poutrida, a pork and cabbage dish, then Nikolas had crossed the cake with a knife and cut it into pieces, offering it first to God, Christ, the Virgin Mary, the house and then sharing it amongst the family starting with the eldest first. They had even plated a piece for Erika's absent husband. This had brought tears to Sophie's eyes as Erika said a small prayer for her lost love and the father of her son's.

Stefano, Anna and the children had returned to their family home in Agia Efimia on the opposite island of Kefalonia as soon as the sea was calm enough, hitching a ride with one of the local fishermen. Their departure created an eerie silence to the house as the children had been such bundles of energy throughout their stay. Sophie had also missed the companionship of Anna, who she had spent so many nights chatting with wrapped in blankets on the veranda and talking until the early hours.

Having someone close to her age to chat with who had also integrated from another culture, had been a blessing as Anna had given her invaluable advice on how to settle and be accepted into the local community of this pretty tradition infused island. Anna had explained how island life could sometimes be very isolating and had a way of sometimes making newcomers feel a little trapped. This was more prevalent through winter, as she had experienced when she first moved there with Stefano, before making a decision to move to the larger island as it had given them more options as a young couple. Having no way off the island for long periods, especially when the boats had cancelled due to rough seas, had sometimes made her feel a bit like a castaway as everywhere was deathly silent. Anna had managed by painting and sketching her way through the darkest months. A hobby she wished she had time for now as a busy mother of three young children. How Sophie had wished that she had had a hobby to while away the long hours.

The festivities had lasted until the sixth day of January, where the cross throwing ceremony symbolised the end of the twelve days of Epiphany. With the church bells tolling, the bay waters rippling in the increased winter winds, the locals emerged from the warmth of their homes and onto the streets of Kioni Bay wrapped in their winter coats. A procession of families chanted and sang their way through the streets accompanied by a local priest, dressed in the finest golden Vestment Sophie had seen, holding onto a wooden cross, as they all made their way to the sea. He had delivered a sermon and then blessed the waters with the cross that he threw into the darkness of the uninviting January Sea.

The air was now cold and the sharp winds had stung at Sophie's face. Pulling her jacket across her chest she had hugged its warmth into her to keep the chill out. A cluster of daring young lads from Kioni, and neighbouring villages braved the chilly temperatures regardless and, using all their inner strength, dived off the seawall in a race to be the first to retrieve it from the depths. The one who emerged from the water with the cross would be blessed with good luck for the remainder of the year.

Panos, the youngest son of a local goat herder, had emerged victorious from the water and was lifted above the heads of his competitors as he claimed his blessing from the priest. This had spilled over to a continuation of celebrations throughout the day involving everyone heading to Spavento bar for coffee followed by more blessings with holy water, singing, more eating, drinking and dancing the coldness away. These evenings always embraced the true Ithacan way of life.

The Christmas celebrations had taken it out of Sophie and increased her weight by at least half a stone, which she vowed to remove before Nikolas returned in spring. But on the upside, Sophie had spent so much time getting to know Maria, chatting together for hours into the night about her childhood memories and future dreams. They had formed quite a bond. After she had said her goodbyes to Nikolas and his daughter, the house had fallen silent with just Erika as company. Even though her host was delightful and made her belly laugh, the thought of another few months without Nikolas had made her heart sink.

Then the snow had arrived. The clouds had been heavy and grey for days before they had scattered the mountaintops with a white dusting, creating a magical winter wonderland in the dark pine trees above. This had made the roads above Kioni treacherous and plummeted the temperatures to below freezing for the first time in years. Sophie had never even considered that she would see snow on an island that she had always considered being hot and sunny. It had only lasted a few days until the blue skies had reappeared and made everything feel more inviting and hopeful. Yet January had brought a deafening silence to the village as the streets had remained empty and people hibernated away from the cold winds that rushed into the bay from across the icy Ionian seas. She had also started to feel the cabin fever that Anna had described and had felt very restricted on what she could do to pass the time without being able to travel to Exoghi to make a start on the house.

As February had approached, the air was becoming a little warmer and the magic of the island was starting to manifest itself deeper into her heart. Sophie had witnessed more blue skies than grey through winter on Ithaca than she would have ever experienced back in the UK. With spring just around the corner, she had also started to shake off the winter blues in anticipation of the return of Nikolas in the coming weeks.

She had celebrated her first Papadis with Erika, with lots of people visiting the village to share in the traditional ceremony. The extravagant interior of the church was magical and shone golden as the taper candles lit up the darkness. With everything said and sung in Greek, Sophie had remained in complete silence and just absorbed every element of the atmospheric ceremony in wonder. Priests wearing beautifully opulent robes had held candles towards the altar, chanted and sang as the congregation watched and joined in where necessary. A display of bread in various baskets was laid out on the floor of the church, all baked as offerings by the women who attended. After the ceremony, they had all gathered to eat the bread that had been blessed by the visiting priests and spent time outside the church, as Erika greeted old friends, introducing Sophie to as many people as possible and chatted the remainder of the night away.

Early spring brought colour to the mountains as the flowers had started to blossom across the island, providing the grazing cattle with delicious fresh shoots to feed on. It had also allowed Sophie to brave the deserted roads and visit Exhogi for the first time in months along with Erika for company and support. Having not been to the village for a while, Sophie stood and looked across Afales Bay below and out over the ocean towards Lefkas.

"This view is out of this world Erika! I can't find the words to describe how beautiful it is!" she exclaimed as she breathed in the freshness of the mountain air.

"That is what Exoghi means, my dear, out of this world, as its beauty is a feast for the eyes and soul. This is why I say that Nikolas has the best view in all of Ithaki!" Erika had responded.

The house had been bitterly cold and uninviting on their first arrival. They had made a log fire just to dry out the dampness in the rooms and create some welcoming warmth before starting the cleaning and discarding the remaining drab furnishings. Having spent the entire day in the bleakness of the forgotten house and to busy to think of eating, Sophie had suddenly felt dizzy and overwhelmed by the pressure of restoring the house without Nikolas. Erika had gathered some Horta from the gardens, that had just looked like dandelions and other weeds to Sophie, and had suggested that they should make their way back to Kioni as they had been so busy and forgotten they had needed to eat. Sophie had driven them back to the inviting warmth and comforts of Philoxenia. On arrival, Erika had created a nourishing soup from the spring greens as Sophie made a list of things she needed to buy to continue with her redecorating before taking a much-needed nap.

After a few further visits in the coming weeks and her efforts of redecorating, sanding and painting, Sophie was pleased with what she saw in front of her. Pulling the dustsheets off the freshly delivered furniture and placing a fresh bouquet of fresh spring flowers on the coffee table, she stood back with a smile. Closing the vibrant blue shutters and pulling the front door closed, she gave a contended smile of achievement, jumped into the car and headed back to Kioni ready for Nikolas' return.

Chapter 3

Having spent all morning at the house, Sophie was exhausted. Erika ran her a relaxing bath pouring a few drops of lavender oil into the steamy water, explaining this would decrease her stress levels and she would smell irresistible for Nikolas.

"It always worked for me when I had been waiting for my love to return from sea," Erika smiled as she left the bathroom with a twinkle in her eye. Sophie discarded her clothes onto the floor and stepped into the warm, inviting water. The heady scent of the lavender calmed her excited mind and she felt her body relax as her thoughts drifted to Nikolas.

A Sophie soaked away her aches, Erika busied herself cooking anticipating the arrival of her family at any moment. Making Spanakopita from the remaining greens she had foraged and a large chunk of feta, Erika sang loudly along with the radio as she continued to bake baklava from the leftover filo pastry. The smell of hot melting cheese, cinnamon and sweet, nutty pastry filled the kitchen with its homely aroma as it cooked ready for her guests.

After getting herself out of the bath and feeling a little nauseous from the heat and overpowering scent, Sophie looked at her reflection in the mirror and scrutinised her voluptuous pear-shaped body. She had not lost the weight that she had intended to before Nikolas had returned. Winter had not allowed her to be as active as she had liked, and Erika's Greek cuisine lessons had seen them eat countless additional calories that she had not accounted for. Disheartened, Sophie pulled her favourite dress over her head, hiding the disappointment of her wobbly frame and wandered downstairs to get a bite to eat. The tempting smells wafting through the house from the kitchen had ignited her palate and made her ravenous as she joined Erika at the kitchen table.

"Beautiful, Sophie! How you feeling? Not long before they arrive! Shall we take coffee outside with some bread and cheese? You must be very hungry, no?" Erika said as Sophie's stomach erupted with an echoing growl of agreement.

"I am pretty hungry, Erika, but it might just be nerves. It has felt so long since I last saw Nikolas. With the winter storms stopping me from travelling to Athens and Nikolas from visiting here, winter has really dragged by," she said, relieved that it was almost over.

"Absence makes the heart love harder, my dear!" Erika exclaimed. "Winter has been hard this year, but we have enjoyed each other's company, no? We are through the worst of it now and the next few weeks will bring us more light and warmer days. Now I will prepare our snack," she said, lifting herself from the kitchen chair.

Sophie grabbed her coat and wandered onto the veranda that looked out over the turquoise hues of the sea. The colours were now coming more alive and inviting as the seasons changed. After all the winter rains, the island was looking a vibrant lush green and coming alive with the return of spring. The faint scent of sage and oregano was again starting to waft in the warming air, returning the island back to how Sophie had remembered from her first visit. The past few days had brought a little more sunshine making the temperatures feel mild and Sophie had noted a few more people braving T-shirts although she had still felt a chill in the air.

Wrapping her self in the warmth of her coat, Sophie took a seat at the garden table as Erika appeared through the doorway, humming contently to herself and carrying a tray of Greek bread, honey, salad and coffee. Setting the light snack on the table, she took a seat next to Sophie and took a slice of the bread, drizzling it with honey.

"You look chlomos, how you say...pale. You need a little Ithaki sunshine to return the glow on those cheeks," Erika said, offering her some of the sticky honey bread. Sophie took a slice and poured a coffee for them both.

"How long do you think they will be? I haven't been able to contact Nikolas yet this morning, and the wait is driving me crazy!" Sophie said impatiently as she took a bite of the bread, which oozed the golden honey down the side of her mouth.

"A little patience, my dear Sophie. Nikolas has to get his boat into the water and check it all over, ready for their first voyage of the year. You do not want him to sink to the bottom of the Ionian Sea, do you?" Erika replied calmly.

"Of course not! I just want them here. I have so much to show Nikolas, and I am excited to take Maria to her birth home. My nerves can't take a moment more waiting!" Sophie replied, trying to dial Nikolas' mobile for the hundredth time that day, and yet again reaching the answerphone. Sophie put the mobile in her lap and looked glumly towards the horizon wishing for her love to return.

"Its no use with the mobile Sophie, Kioni has hardly any signal unless you wander high up the hillside. There you will probably see him on the water anyway!" Erika smiled.

Nikolas had spent all morning trying to get through to Sophie, but every time, the mobile had connected straight to her answerphone.

"When will they get a better signal in Kioni!" he said, throwing his phone in frustration into the pile of ropes that lay coiled on the deck of Evangeline. He concentrated his frustration on servicing the boat engine ahead of their first trip at sea since September the previous year. Having watched them lower his pride and joy into the water that morning after a thorough check of her hull, Nikolas had sprung into action, ensuring the boat was safe on the water for the fishing season ahead. This had taken him a lot longer than he had anticipated as he had encountered a problem calibrating his new depth sounder. This was the one instrument he needed to be in full working order so he could navigate the seabed and avoid ripping a hole in the hull on the rocks hidden below sea level.

Maria had patiently sat watching her Papa as he worked as swiftly as possible. She had flicked through her numerous social media accounts over and over and was now sat happily chatting on face time to her boyfriend in Athens. Nikolas smiled at his daughters face lighting up with a warm glow of young innocent love. He was so desperate to be back in the arms of Sophie, who was right at that moment, awaiting his arrival on the island he could see across the water. Regardless of his desires, he couldn't rush the process as a slight overlook could be disastrous. The distance between them seemed so vast at that moment as he became frustrated with the slightest delay to his eager return. With the last few checks completed, including checking the fuel lines for cracks and the engine coolant levels, Nikolas started up the engine creating a small bellow of smoke from the protective oil he had sprayed over the engine before winter.

Checking the oil levels and happy with the water flow, he shone his torch into the engine bay to check for any obvious leaks and listened carefully for any strange sounds that may have indicated a problem. With his GPS system now working perfectly, Nikolas smiled at the sound of Evangeline that purred its trusty reliability back at him. Shouting to Maria to climb on board, Nikolas instructed her to untie the mooring ropes. He gently pushed the throttle and felt Evangeline pull away from the dock.

This feeling sent a sense of excitement and freedom through Nikolas's veins as he pointed the boat in the direction of Ithaca. This is where he felt peace and was at his happiest, he thought to himself, as Evangeline cut through the waves sending a salty spray over the face of Maria, who was sat at the stern of the boat. Turning to see his daughter shrieking and smiling as she had done as a child, softened Nikolas's heart and brought a tear to his eyes. How he had missed his daughter's company on his sea adventurers. The pure enjoyment of the spray tickling her face reminded him of Sophie's first trip on his boat the year previous and how she had reminded him of his Maria. Sophie. A sudden urge to hold her in his arms filled his soul. How he had missed this beautiful woman who had stolen his heart and brought purpose to his life again.

Winter in Athens had been so lonely and tiring as he had worked at the factory by day and the bars at night just to make enough money to cover his winter expenses on Kefalonia. He had also managed to save enough money to start rebuilding the swimming pool as his home on Ithaca as a gift for Sophie. But the time away from Sophie had been hard. Hearing her crying her loneliness down the phone and not being able to hold her had broken his heart over and over.

The many times he had tried to get a flight or ferry back to the island only to be cancelled and turned away due to the weather had been frustrating. Ithaca was cut off from the rest of the world through winter, but it had not been a bother in the past as he had not needed to return. But with his heart being left on the island, he had felt incomplete and had wanted to return to the warmth of his lover's arms. As Evangeline skirted the coastline of Ithaca, passing by Gidaki beach, Nikolas felt the excitement pounding in his chest. Just a little longer and he would be cruising through the small opening of Kioni Bay and he would be with his Sophie again at last.

Sophie was so restless. She couldn't contain her excitement as she scanned the horizon. With every boat that headed into the bay, her heart lifted and then sank with disappointment as another unfamiliar craft glided by. Erika had headed into the house and was frantically cleaning ready for the impending arrival of her son and granddaughter. The smell of the spices from the warming Spanakopita, wafted onto the veranda and filled Sophie with a sudden comfortable feeling of being home. It was the first time she had actually felt this sensation in the whole time she had been on Ithaca. The island now felt like home.

The cry of a cat on the pebbly shore below the house distracted Sophie's attention for a split second as she observed it watching a fish swimming in the shallows of the cove. Its frustration mimicked how Sophie had felt right at that moment knowing that pure happiness and contentment was just beyond her reach but out there on the water. She smiled as it refused to leap into the waters to capture the tasty meal that tempted its primal hunting instincts. As she continued to watch its comical attempts at dipping its paws into the sea to catch the elusive meal, she faintly heard her name called from across the waves.

Sophie's heart leapt as a familiar voice reached her with the sea breeze. She jerked her eyes onto the horizon to see a blue and white boat chugging its way around the headland and into the bay. She could not contain her excitement and shouted to Erika to join her. Rushing through the door, Erika and Sophie both hugged each other and waved frantically at the safe arrival of Nikolas and Maria. Tears streamed down Sophie's face in relief from her frustration as Nikolas waved his arms and blew her kisses as he glided passed the house.

Unable to wait a moment longer, Sophie made her way swiftly to the harbour in time to greet Nikolas and Maria as they both worked in complete unison to dock Evangeline. It was so evident that Maria had spent so much time with her father on the boat as a young child as she tied the mooring line to the harbour side cleat without any need for instruction from Nikolas.

Sophie must have radiated happiness as Nikolas jumped off Evangeline and picked her up in his powerful arms, spinning her around before sinking his lips against hers. She melted into his embrace and felt tears of every emotion run down her cheeks as Nikolas wrapped his protective arms around her, pulling her deeply into his chest.

"I have missed you so much, my Sophie!" he whispered into her ear, sending shivers down her spine. "I never want to be without you for that long again. Next time if I leave, you will come with me, endaxi!"

Sophie couldn't speak between her sobs of joy, so she just gave a nod as a smile spread across her face.

"Put her down, your way to old to behave like that Papa!" smiled Maria, as she followed her father off the boat.

"You are never to old for romance, Maria!" said Sophie, after taking a few breaths to compose herself and wiping the tears from her eyes. Spreading her arms out, she pulled Maria into a hug and kissed her on both cheeks. "How has your journey been? You must be so hungry as it's after lunch. Are you hungry? I hope so as Erika has made her usual feast for us all and is so excited to see you both. Shall we make our way back?" Sophie inquired.

"Slow down with your hurried words, agapi mou! We need to collect our bags, and then we will be good to go!" Nikolas smiled, as he remembered how endearing Sophie was when she became excited.

Sophie gave Nikolas an apologetic warm smile as she linked her arm into Maria's and started to slowly stroll ahead, leaving Nikolas weighed down with several bags stuffed to near bursting point with his daughter's clothes.

"Why you need so much stuff, Maria? You are here for only a few days, or are you back for good?" Nikolas mocked.

"Papa, a lady needs lots of clothes and all the essentials as who knows what may happen. I am going to visit Theia Anna before I fly home, remember, so I needed extra as we might go to Argostoli shopping and for a night out with my friends, no?!" she replied.

How had his little girl grown up so fast, Nikolas thought to himself whilst struggling to maintain control of his baggage as they walked along the winding road to Philoxenia.

As Sophie pushed open the garden gate, they were immediately greeted by a tearful Erika, who pulled Maria into a warm embrace and kissed her over and over on both cheeks, before eventually letting her go. Then, without giving Nikolas a chance to offload the heavy baggage, she launched a welcoming embrace on her son.

"It is so good to have my family home! Ella, Ella! Come, Come!" Erika insisted as she turned and ushered everyone to the rear of the house. "Your room is all ready for you, Maria. Take your bags and come down for lunch. I have your favourite, Baklava," she smiled as she turned to see Nikolas and Sophie locked in an embrace. "You don't need to eat each other! I have plenty of food if you are hungry?" Erika laughed as she headed for the kitchen, leaving them to a moment of privacy.

"I can't believe that you are here. I have been feeling sick all morning with nerves waiting for your boat to return. I am just so glad that you are back. Winter has been so hard without you here Nikolas. Please don't leave me again, promise?" Sophie said grabbing hold of Nikolas's hand and wandering to take a seat at the table.

"My beautiful Sophie. It has been hard for me also hearing your sadness on the telephone and not being able to hold you. It has broken my heart over and over. I will never leave you again, I promise. I love you so much and am so excited for our future," he replied.

At that moment, Maria wandered onto the veranda carrying a stack of plates and cutlery followed by Erika holding a tray of glasses and a carafe of wine. Then returning back inside with Maria, emerging with the now warmed Spanakopita, a Greek salad and basket of seeded bread rolls. Taking a seat to join Nikolas and Sophie, Erika sliced the steamy pie making it crunch under the blade. The scent of freshly baked pastry, the pungent aroma of melted feta and warm spices of cinnamon wafted across the table as they enjoyed their first meal together in months blessed by the warm spring sunshine.

Chapter 4

Having spent a few hours catching up and with Sophie's constant pestering to visit the house in Exoghi, Nikolas gave in. Jumping into the car, they headed up the mountain road that followed the coastline to the north of the island.

Sophie loved being back in the car alongside Nikolas. It reminded her of their first adventures together on Kefalonia and how he had been her elected tour guide before their relationship had taken a different turn. The day Nikolas had saved her from drowning in the turquoise waters of Assos, had been a defining moment in her life. It had been the moment that she had felt a deeper connection to the man who now held her hand as they drove to their first home together.

As they approached the gates to the house, Sophie turned to look at Maria, who was looking a little uncomfortable in the back of the car.

"Are you OK, Maria? I know it must be hard to come here after all these years. Its beauty really is a contrast to your mother's presence here. Come, let us take a look around," she said, reassuringly.

Stepping out of the parked car, Nikolas was instantly taken back by the amount of work Sophie had achieved in just the gardens alone.

"Sophie, it's incredible! You have worked so hard here. The house, it looks so.....loved. I cannot thank you enough for this," he said, pulling her into his arms.

"It really hasn't taken that long, and with Erika's help to make sure that I wasn't removing anything I shouldn't. The gardens were pretty much matured and just hidden under years of neglect. I found a beautiful old tree at the bottom of the terrace with incredible uninterrupted views over the bay. It will be such a lovely place to sit out of the sun," she advised.

"That is the white Jasmine tree that Evangeline's Papa planted when she was firstborn. I have not seen it for a very long time. It is a beautiful place to spend an evening under the scent of its pure white flowers. I will make a bench there for us to enjoy the sunsets together with a glass of wine," he smiled as he pulled Sophie into his lips. "I am the luckiest man alive! Come, Maria, I will show you around!" Nikolas called to his daughter.

Following everyone to the rear of the house, Sophie could see Maria's eyes light up as the expanse of the view opened up before her.

"Papa, it is so beautiful here. Is this really where I was born? Why have I not seen it before today? The views are just incredible! Can we go inside?" questioned Maria.

"So many questions with answers that are filled with guilt, Maria, but maybe I can try to explain after we have had a look around, no?" Nikolas replied, with the pressure of the moment surging inside his heart.

Sophie had already unlocked the freshly painted doors into the family home, leaving Nikolas and Maria to visit her past together. Taking a seat next to Erika under the grapevine, she hoped that she had created the perfect memory for Maria of her first visit to her birth home.

"Do you think that it all looks OK, Erika. Have I been gentle with Evangeline's memory, or should I have left it as it was until after she had seen it?" questioned Sophie.

"You worry too much, my dear Sophie!" Erika stated. "You have brought this house back to life and shown respect for Maria in everything you have done. I am sure Nikolas will agree. You have such a kind heart," reassured Erika.

"I just want it to be perfect for her, Erika. This must be so hard to digest. A house that has so many important memories, hidden from her for her entire life. I hope that she sees how loved she would have been by her mother if things had been different. I can't imagine how life has been for Maria, not ever knowing her mother. I know she has had you and Anna to fill that void, but it is not the same. That perfect nursery was created by a mother's pure love for her unborn child. I have dreamt of experiencing that all my life but will now never have that chance. My age is battling with my maternal desires," She said solemnly.

"Life has a plan for us all, Sophie. Nothing happens by fate alone. You were meant to feel the pain you did and come to Ithaki to meet Nikolas. Who knows what the stars have planned for you both next!" exclaimed Erika. "Come, let us take a walk and leave them to it. They will join us when they are ready."

Nikolas followed Maria into the living room of the freshly decorated home. Everything felt so different, yet it had not changed too much, removing his memories of Evangeline. Everything was just perfect. Even Evangeline's picture from his home in Sami now hung on the perfectly painted white walls of the house they had once shared. He could hardly contain his emotions as his respect for Sophie surged, knowing that it must be so hard for her to share a home with his late wife's ghost. He watched in silence as Maria wandered around the room and absorbed as much detail as possible from her surroundings.

"This was your grandparent's home too, Maria. Generations of your Mama's family have lived in this house. I am so sorry it has taken so long for you to visit. I just could not face the pain this house caused me. It was very selfish of me," he said, breaking the silence.

"It's okay, Papa. I do not feel resentment for you not bringing me here. I understand how much pain it would have brought you. I remember much more than you know from being a little girl. I remember hearing you cry for Mama when you thought I was asleep. I blamed myself for her death and wished that I could make you happy. I knew how much you loved and missed her," she said, looking at her mother's picture on the wall.

"You were not to blame for her death. How can you think this? You always did make me happy and still do, Maria. It was you that made me strong enough to get through each day. Your eyes carried your Mama's heart, and I could see her looking back at me through your soul. I blamed myself for many years, and that guilt has been so heavy on my mind. But I have to let it go now. I cannot keep living in the shadows of my past, our past. This house holds our memories good and bad, and they need celebrating, not forgetting. Sophie has taught me this," he smiled as he followed Maria into the hallway.

Opening the door to the nursery, Maria stepped into the pink room. Everything had been left untouched by Sophie and was very much as Evangeline had left it ready for the arrival of her first child. The wooden nursing chair sat forlorn next to the wicker cradle, looking out towards the serenity of the mountains beyond. Her unworn baby clothes were still untouched and perfectly folded on the changing unit. A forgotten floppy pink bunny still lay in an empty wicker cradle waiting to meet its new playmate. A playmate that had now arrived after almost twenty years of waiting. Maria reached into the cradle and lifted the bunny to her chest. She breathed in the musky scent of time. Closing her eyes, she felt herself well up inside. All those years of longing to be close to the woman who had given her life for her's. A hole that had never really been filled by anyone. She had hidden a silent desire to be close to her Mama but not wanting to upset her Papa as she had seen his pain at the very mention of her name. The room had shown how much she had been wanted and how much her mother would have loved her. Every detail had been planned so perfectly.

She pushed the familiar pain back inside and gave the seagull mobile over the crib a gentle push sending it peacefully around in a circle. A smile pushed across her face as for the first time, she felt a deep connection to her Mama. Maria almost felt her presence in the shrine that had been created from her loss.

Nikolas had remained in the doorway and observed his daughter in silence, giving her the time to absorb everything she needed. He understood the magnitude of different emotions that she would be experiencing and the time it needed to be digested. He watched her as she explored a room that his late wife had spent so many hours creating to complete perfection for a baby that she had been so desperate to meet. That baby was now seeing her mother's love for the first time in almost twenty years.

Tears ran down his face as he watched as Maria picked up the pink bunny from the cradle. He remembered that Evangeline had bought the floppy teddy during a trip to the neighbouring island of Zakynthos after she had found out that she was pregnant. It had been the very first baby item that she had bought as she had been so sure from day one that she had been carrying a girl. He could visualise her excitement with her first purchase. Her beautiful eyes had sparkled and a perfect smile had radiated across her glowing face. Seeing that bunny in Maria's arms after all that time, was almost too painful for Nikolas to cope with as visions of his Evangeline filled his mind. Retreating from the doorway, Nikolas gave himself a moment to compose before Maria turned and faced his pained gaze.

Without a word spoken, Maria threw her arms around her Papa, needing to feel the comfort of his protective arms. For a few moments, they remained in complete silence. Words were not required to provide the support they both needed from the intensity of the grief they both shared. Maria soaked her Papa's shirt as she let all the years of pain out with every tear. Maria had not really considered how the visit would affect her. She had often wondered if she would be happy or sad about the memories that this secret house would unlock. Now, being surrounded by the display of love that her Mama had for her unborn child, it was too overwhelming and deeply painful.

Maria pulled away from her Papa without meeting his gaze and pushed open the doorway to the opposite bedroom. A white dressing table sat looking out towards the mountains. It was covered with her Mama's jewellery, makeup and a half full bottle of perfume. Maria wandered into the room and sat down on the dressing table stool. She stared at her reflection in the mirror. A mirror that her Mama had once gazed into and a seat that she had once sat on. Having been told all her life that she was her living double, Maria wondered what her Mama would look like now if she had not been taken from them. She reluctantly reached out for her hairbrush that had sat untouched for years on the dressing table top. Holding the brush in her hands, Maria felt the imprints of her Mama's memory surge through her veins. It was almost as if her existence was confirmed by the presence of her hair tangled in its bristles.

Maria had no memory of her Mama's side of the family as her grandparents had passed away when she was still so very young and her Mama had been an only child. This had meant there were no childhood stories from family to fill the void of her loss. Her Mother had often felt like a stranger to her and for this, she had always felt guilty. Spraying her Mama's perfume onto her skin, she inhaled the light pleasant flora aroma that sent tingles of sadness through her body. This is how her Mama had smelt, she thought as tears filled her eyes. This unfamiliar smell would have been the catalyst to her past and instantly regressed her to her childhood no matter where she had smelt it. The very scent that would have intoxicated her as her Mama had wrapped her arms around her, smothered her in comfort pulling her deep into her warmth and filling her senses with love. A smell that should have been ingrained in her memory for a lifetime. Placing the perfume into her pocket, she continued to look through her Mama's belongings as Nikolas stood watching from the doorway.

Watching Maria sat at the dressing table was almost like seeing his Evangeline's ghost staring back at him through the mirror. The resemblance was so incredible in every way, the hair, the skin, the features and the height. Maria was almost a mirror image of his lost love. As the scent of the perfume wafted through the air, Nikolas inhaled its familiar aroma and felt it reach his deepest memories. At that very moment he could not take anymore. Feeling his pain surging uncontrollably through his body, Nikolas needed air. In desperation, he stumbled his way along the passageway, almost vomiting with the sudden anguish. Finally, reaching the open doors to the patio, he stood in the doorway and took a few breaths just to try to regain control of his emotions. The calming scent of the sage and rosemary filled his lungs, and after a few moments, he felt his heart rate return too normal. Nikolas searched the gardens with his eyes for Sophie. He needed to feel her presence and be close to her.

Eventually, hearing voices from the terraces below, Nikolas left Maria with her thoughts and headed to find Sophie. Being in the gardens removed the suppression of his anguish and filled his heart with peace as Sophie came into view. Reaching for her from behind, Nikolas hugged her deep into his chest and breathed in her scent. That connection removed his sadness and reminded him that his future was in his arms at that very moment. His past was not something that would ever leave him, but he had to let go of his guilt and focus on Sophie.

"Hey! You made me jump creeping up on me like that!" Sophie said softly and let herself sink into his sudden embrace. Feeling his intensity and tenseness of his body, Sophie knew that something had happened. "Is everything OK, Nikolas? How did things go with Maria?"

"Seeing my Maria sat where her Mama once sat was like seeing a ghost. I needed to get some air and to feel you close to me. But now that I am with you, everything is gone. It is all better again." he replied. "Maria is sat with her Mama's belongings. Thank you for this, Sophie. You are an incredible woman, and I am so grateful that you allowed Maria the chance to connect with her Mama. I would have understood if you wanted to remove everything for a fresh start. But what you have shown me is more of the wonderful woman that I fall in love with more each day."

33

"I would never have imposed myself on Maria. Today is so essential for her own healing, we have plenty of time to change things for us!" replied Sophie.

"And this is what makes you special, Sophie!" exclaimed Erika. "You have the heart of an angel and soul of a wise old lady!" she continued with a smile. "I will go check on Maria and leave you to love birds alone for a few moments" And with that, she disappeared behind the rosemary bushes.

Nikolas took Sophie's hand and led her along the pathway to a viewpoint that looked out over the green vistas down towards Afales Beach and over the wild blue sea. It's breath taking beauty always took her by surprise as she scanned the horizon before her and again had to remind herself that this was now home.

"What are the pyramids for?" she questioned as she noted three triangular stones stood prominently on the outskirts of Exhogi village.

"These are tombs. Two were built to bury an eccentric builder and his Mama back in the 1930s. The third tomb is someone unknown. At night they light up the hillside and can be seen from afar. I will take you for a visit to Exhogi one day soon. It is a pretty special place, one of the oldest villages on Ithaki and full of history. Odysseus Palace, the School of Homer, is also here a little closer to the village of Stavros. We were taught about it in school. I have so much to share with you." He smiled, remembering how much Sophie loved his stories.

"I cannot quite believe that I actually live here. I feel as though this is all a dream still," she said, closing her eyes and breathing in the warm aromatics of marjoram and thyme that carpeted the surrounding scrubland. "I look forward to you telling me more about our home and visiting the villages," replied Sophie.

At that moment, Erika and Maria emerged from the undergrowth to join them. Maria's eyes were puffy and reddened. She remained in complete silence as Nikolas walked towards her and pulled her into his embrace.

"Come, let us head back to Philoxenia. It's the start of the Apokries so we will celebrate with the rest of the island for the next few weeks," Erika said, with a broad smile across her face.

Chapter 5

Having spent a few more days with Maria at the house, packing away the memories of Evangeline, Sophie started to feel a bit more relaxed. She no longer felt the need to share the house with the ghost of her predecessor. Maria had carefully placed her Mother's belongings into a pretty wooden carved box that Erika had gifted, and taken them back to Philoxenia along with the floppy pink bunny from her unused crib. This had allowed Sophie a chance to reclaim the bedroom and start to place her own feminine stamp on the room.

They celebrated the festival of Tsiknopempti with the rest of the village, helping to string up bunting across the old village school and set up the tables and chairs. The taverna's opened their doors and villagers set up several barbeque drums around the playground. The smell of smoky charcoal filled the air as grilled and roasted meats of all kinds sizzled on the griddles. Whoever wasn't nursing a seasonal cold headed to this important celebration that was alive with the deafening vibrations of children's screeches and laughter. The men came dressed up as women and women dressed up as vixens, sporting headbands with little ears poking out from their hair. Even though the sky was clear there was still a cold chill in the air. Everyone wrapped in their warm coats or thick jumpers, even though misleading summer blue skies welcomed everyone who came along to join in the Thursday celebration of Kreatini, ahead of Lent.

After they had recovered from the celebrations Nikolas and Sophie spent the next day clearing the terraces of the garden at the villa and exposed more hidden pathways from the overgrowth. As promised, Nikolas made a bench and created a small barbeque area for them to enjoy an outdoor meal under the intoxicating scent of its delicate white flowers. They spent Maria's last evening on Ithaca at the house in Exhogi. Sat out under the Jasmine tree, the three of them enjoyed the picture-postcard views of the landscape, while sharing a bottle of wine and watching the apocalyptic hues of the departing sun over the horizon until darkness had settled for the night.

"We still have no name for the house," said Sophie, breaking the silence as she watched the magenta of the evening skies change to deep violet.

"It has an ancient name that suits it perfectly. This house has stood watching over these seas for hundreds of years as far back as the 1700s. This has always been known as Villa Elysian because it almost feels like you have found paradise and could never become any happier," Nikolas replied.

"What does Elysian mean?" questioned Sophie.

"Elysian is a paradise where good men, blessed by the gods, would be sent to spend their afterlife. Like ancient Greek heaven for mortals, ruled by Hades, the Greek God of the underworld. Here on Ithaca, Homer told of the Elysian Plains in his poetry. Let me see if I can remember from my childhood teachings," he said, clearing his throat before continuing in a powerful and profound, melodic voice, "A place where men lead an easier life than anywhere else in the world. For in Elysium, there falls not rain, nor hail, nor snow, but Oceanus breathes ever with a West wind that sings softly from the sea and gives fresh life to all men," Nikolas quoted, proud of his unfailing memory.

"Well, I believe that is the most perfect name for this house. It is most definitely a paradise that I would be happy to spend an eternity in, although it does rain and snow a bit more than I had anticipated!" Sophie said, impressed yet again by his knowledge.

"I remember being taught that in school, Papa!" Maria added. "Why is the name not on the gate or house?"

"I had intended to have it carved into stone by a friend in the neighbouring village, but he passed away a few years ago. I will have it sorted so we can enjoy our very own Elysian plain every night watching over the Ionian Seas like the Gods before us," he said, standing up from the bench. "Come, let us head back to Philoxenia to enjoy the last meal of Tsiknopemti, and so we can get you packed and ready for Theia Anna's tomorrow Maria."

As they both followed behind Nikolas toward the illuminating warmth of the stone house that she now knew as Villa Elysian, Sophie felt in awe of the ancient history that she had become a part of. Ancient Greece had always seemed a bit more interesting than that of British history, as depicted by the many films she had watched as a child. A magical country, with its modern world, created from supernatural, mythological creatures and Gods that built an empire for the present-day Greek culture and still remained deeply rooted in their beliefs as she had witnessed through her stay with Erika.

The only comparison that she could make with British history was that of the ancient Welsh mythological tales of King Arthur and his sorcerer, Merlin. Tales told to her by her Welsh grandparents during her annual weekly stay on the wild and windy shores of Pembrokeshire. Bedtime stories told of Welsh fairy folk and the underworld of Annwn, similar to that of Elysian. These tales had ignited her imagination and made those childhood holidays so much more exciting at the thought of the ancient magic that possibly surrounded her as she played in the woodland's searching for the existence of fairies or a magical sword in a stone.

As Nikolas locked up Villa Elysian, Sophie took a seat in the darkness of the car with Maria and wound down the window allowing the fresh evening scent of the rosemary to waft into the staleness as they waited.

"I can't wait to come back to visit again, Sophie. Thank you for what you did for me. It meant the world that you left Mama's belongings for me to see. I don't think it would have been the same if you had just handed them to me in a box. Having a chance to walk in her footsteps and sit in her memories has been so healing for me. I can see why Papa loves you so much. You really are such a special lady, and I would be happy for you to become part of our family. Papa is so much happier now. I never thought I would see him smile again as much as he does when he is with you," said Maria.

"It wasn't a problem, Maria. I understand how important it would have been for you to see your childhood home as it was. There is plenty of time for a change. I am not here to take any of your mother's memories away. I wanted you to spend time with her before we changed a thing. I would never have been able to live with myself if I had taken that away from you. I hope you will come back and visit us as often as you can. Your Papa also makes me so happy. I feel like I have found my own paradise with him by my side, Villa Elysian or not!" she smiled as Nikolas opened the driver's door.

"Have I missed anything?" he said, as he saw both Sophie and Maria smiling at him as he took a seat.

"You haven't missed a thing, just girl talk Papa!" said Maria giving him a hug from behind and a kiss to his cheek. "Thank you for a wonderful time and for showing me our very own piece of paradise. I was just telling Sophie how I can't wait to return to visit you both!"

"Maybe we will have your bedroom changed, so it is more fitting with your age. I guess pretty pink is not quite right for you any longer, No?" Nikolas said, placing his hand on Sophie's thigh.

"Who knows, you might need to keep it as a nursery!" she winked, as both Sophie and Nikolas looked back at her in shock.

"I think I am a bit too old for that now, Maria! My time has gone, and maybe your children will come first," Sophie responded, with a longing smile.

As they travelled back along the roads towards Kioni, the waterfront lights of Frikes Bay twinkled in the distance below, creating a romantic atmosphere to the once darker winter landscape. The island was starting to come alive with the start of spring, Easter was fast approaching and the gradual return of the tourist season crept life into the islands sleepy winter hibernation.

Sophie turned to look at Nikolas as they drove the mountain roads. His silhouette perfectly framed by the brightness of the full moon that bathed the clear night sky. She felt so happy at that moment. It almost felt that she could not be any happier. Everything felt perfect, and life seemed to be so peaceful. She no longer craved her childhood dream. All she wanted was to be by Nikolas's side. As they dropped down towards Kioni, Sophie watched as the ocean waves that lapped towards the harbour, glimmered in the creaminess of the moonlight. The car came to a gradual halt outside Philoxenia, and Sophie opened her door, allowing the slight warmth of the evening to engulf her. As she stood up, a sudden light-headedness made her fall back onto the car seat.

"Are you OK, Sophie?" said Nikolas as he rushed to help her out.

"I think I am a bit tipsy after the wine. Maybe some of Erika's home-baked bread will soak up the alcohol!" she said, feeling a little peckish. "It has been a little while since we ate, and I seem to be constantly hungry since moving here. I blame all the delicious food Erika has been feeding me, and the constant smell of baking in the air. How can anyone resist the aromatic smells of cinnamon, nutmeg and oregano!" she exclaimed, defending her newfound love of food.

"Mama's food has everyone feeling this way!" replied Nikolas. "Come, let us get you indoors and fed'" he said, taking her by the waist and helping her from the car.

Maria walked ahead and pushed open the garden gate that led to the rear of the house, followed closely by Sophie and Nikolas. Erika was singing away to herself in the warmth of the kitchen as they all descended in through the front door. The smell of sweet tomatoes infused with garlic, filled the air as a pan bubbled away in the far corner of the kitchen, spitting out occasional teasers of its contents. Erika was happily kneading dough on the kitchen table, her face covered in a dusting of flour as she rolled out several flatbreads, covering them in a buttery garlic and sprinkling each with a handful of fresh curly parsley.

"I hope everyone is hungry! I have made our last meat meal of Tserepa. The flatbread will take just a little while longer, so go get yourselves freshened up whilst I prepare the table! Go! Go!" she said, ushering them all out of the kitchen.

Sophie made her way upstairs to change out of her grubby clothes. She still felt a little lightheaded, her abdomen ached, and she felt bloated. Putting it down to being almost that "lady-time of the month," she took a few delicious moments of rest on the bed before she heard her name being called to join them all at the table. With her eyes reluctant to open and body so comfortable, she really felt she could have fallen to sleep for the remainder of the evening. At that moment, Nikolas appeared around the bedroom door to see where Sophie had got to.

"Endaxi Re? You OK? You are looking very pale tonight, Sophie. Maybe you are coming down with something, and a visit by the doctor is needed," Nikolas suggested, with a concerned tone in his voice.

"I just need something to eat and a good rest. I will be absolutely fine. It has been a full-on couple of days work at the Villa and the village celebrations. All the lifting and carrying has tired me out. I am sure that I will be OK. Don't worry so much, Nikolas," she replied, pushing herself up off the bed to join everyone downstairs.

Erika had the table laid out perfectly and decorated with flowers, all ready for Maria's final meal before heading to Kefalonia. Having settled down to enjoy a salad starter with the flatbreads, Erika served the Tserepa and passed the filled plates along the table until everyone had a dish. Sophie looked at the delicious meal in front of her. A leg of perfectly cooked chicken sat on a bed of sliced potatoes and was topped in the thick sweet tomatoes and green pepper sauce. A sprinkle of freshly picked oregano decorated the mouth-watering dish.

"YiaYia!! This is my most favourite meal. You are spoiling me before I leave!" exclaimed Maria, as she tucked into her plate of food.

Sophie placed her knife and fork into the tender, succulent meat, which effortlessly fell from the bone. Putting a forkful of the plate's contents into her mouth, the food seemed to melt before she had a chance to really enjoy the fullness of the individual flavours. Erika's cooking never disappointed and every night had become a Master chef experience for Sophie as she tasted each new traditional meal all worthy of a high-end Greek restaurant.

But tonight, instead of the flavours delighting her taste buds, she felt queasy. She tried a few more mouthful and forced them down without seeming rude. But she couldn't keep it down. In a state of panic, Sophie stood up abruptly, forcibly pushing the chair backward, sending it crashing to the slate floor below. Without any explanation to the shocked faces that sat staring at her, she turned and made a dash upstairs to the safety of the bathroom.

"Sophie! Let me in! Is everything OK?" came Nikolas concerned voice.

Having emptied the contents of her stomach several times, Sophie pulled her head from inside the toilet basin and sat back on the floor, feeling a little clammy but much better now that the flavour of the sweet tomatoes had left her palate.

"Give me a few minutes to freshen myself and I will be out," she said, pushing herself up from the ground to swill her mouth from the cold water tap. Her body ached everywhere, and her head pounded from the retching. She hadn't been sick without it being alcohol-induced in such a long time and remembered how much she had hated the feeling. Hangover sickness generally followed a damn good night out with her girlfriends and had a genuine excuse, but stomach bug sickness was so pointless.

After a few more moments to ensure that she no longer needed the safety of the toilet, Sophie unlocked the bathroom door and stepped out to see a concerned Nikolas sat on the floor. Seeing Sophie, he sprung upwards to check how she was.

"Are you sure that you are OK, Sophie? Shall I call for the doctor to check over you? I think you should take a rest for the evening. I will bring up some water and bread. Mama always gives us bread to soak up the bugs," Nikolas said as he took her by the waist and walked her to their bedroom.

"I will be fine, Nikolas. I will be fighting fit by the morning. A good rest will do me wonders!" Sophie replied as she sat on the bed and slipped off her trousers. "Please apologise to Erika for me. I did not mean to leave the table so abruptly. I just panicked," she said remorsefully.

"Mama does not care for that. As long as you are ok is all that matters. Take a rest, and I will be back with some water," he said, kissing her forehead and leaving the room.

Sophie threw back the bedcovers, turned off the lamp and slipped under the sheet. The coolness of the bed linen against her clammy skin was so soothing. The bed felt so comfortable as she sank into the softness of the pillows. The room was dark, and the moonlight shone in through the open window. Her head pounded, her stomach still ached, and the queasiness remained. She cradled her arms over her bloated belly and considered what might have upset her stomach. She hadn't eaten anything different from Nikolas and he was fine. She didn't have a temperature so she couldn't have a fever so she must be due her period. She thought about when her last cycle was and a sudden realisation erupted from inside. She hadn't had a clue when her last period had been.

With the excitement of everything going on, she hadn't even really noticed anything a miss. She had a feeling she wasn't ill at all.

Sophie lay in the bed in complete disbelief. How could she have overlooked something so simple? Switching on the bedside lamp, she rifled through her drawer to find her personal diary. Here she kept a record of everything, including the start and end dates of every period she had ever had since she was sixteen. Locating the small book at the rear of the drawer, she quickly turned to the notes section and followed the dates downwards with her index finger.

The last date she had recorded was back in December just before Nikolas had returned to Ithaca for Christmas. That would mean that she could be about 10 weeks pregnant. She had to get a pregnancy test to confirm if it was right before she broke the news to Nikolas. But with everyone in the village now knowing her, how would it be possible to buy a testing kit and keeping it a secret. It would be the gossip of the town before she had even returned back to Philoxenia. That was unless she accompanied him to Agia Efimia on Evangeline the next day. Then she could sneak into one of the supermarkets and buy one without anyone knowing her. That was the only thing she could think of.

Flicking the bedside lamp off, she lay in complete silence as the darkness swallowed her vision. A wide smile spread across her face as she placed her hand tenderly against her abdomen. A baby, she thought. But not just any baby. There actually might be Nikolas's child inside her at that very moment. How on earth was she going to keep this to herself all night?

Chapter 6

Sophie woke early the next morning, and, after a further moment of retching into the toilet basin, she jumped into the shower, leaving Nikolas fast asleep in bed. The queasiness had not settled overnight as she had hoped, but she was determined to look well enough to join Nikolas on his trip to Kefalonia. The warmth of the shower eased her aching back, but the hot steam made her feel lightheaded again, and she only remained in the shower spray just long enough to cleanse herself.

As she dried herself off with the softness of a freshly folded towel, she checked her naked reflection in the mirror to see if there was any sign of a giveaway bump that would suggest her thoughts were accurate. She checked over her shoulder to make sure that Nikolas was still fast asleep as she turned from side to side and rubbed her slightly bloated belly. It was so hard to tell as she had piled on so much weight from her new Greek diet and lack of regular exercise. How she wished she was pregnant. She couldn't think of a more perfect man to father her child. She felt her cheeks tighten as a smile spread across her face.

"What a gift for my eyes to wake up to!" came a voice from behind her. Sophie jumped from the sudden sound and turned to see Nikolas sat up in bed, staring at her naked body. "You are such a beautiful woman, Sophie. Every inch of you is so perfect. I am a lucky man," he said as he lent forward and pulled her nakedness into his. Taking her hard nipple into his mouth, he playfully suckled and gently caressed her breast, causing him to become aroused. "How are you feeling this morning?" he remembered, with a pang of slight guilt from his thoughtless advances.

"Much better," she lied, as she hid a wince of pain from the slight tenderness of her breasts and battled with the sick feeling bubbling inside her. "I thought maybe I would join you and Maria this morning and come to Agia Efimia. I have been on Ithaca now for such a long time without leaving, it would be so good to see somewhere different," she said, in a most convincing manner.

45

"Are you sure, Sophie? Maybe you should stay here today and I will take you on a boat trip in a few days. It will give your body time to recover from last night, no?" he suggested.

"I am feeling so much better and the sea air will do me so much good, plus, if I am unwell, I can see a doctor on Kefalonia much easier than on Ithaca," she reminded Nikolas.

"This is very true. The one downside of living on such a small island is just one doctor to see all 3500 inhabitants," he agreed. "Endaxi, you will come with us for the day, and I can keep an eye on you, agreed?"

"Agreed!" Sophie replied with a secret smile. Mission complete, she thought to herself smugly as she continued to dry herself and get dressed.

Sophie made her way downstairs and headed straight out onto the veranda to get some air. With it now being early March, the morning sunshine was starting to rise a little higher in the sky as it reached over the mountain and onto the gardens of Philoxenia. Sophie took a deep breath of the salty sea breeze that wafted across the bay and filled her lungs. Its freshness seemed to bring a momentary stillness to the nausea, just as Erika arrived, holding a cup of strong black coffee.

"Kalimera! How you feel this morning Sophie? I brought your usual morning coffee. It might help you feel better after a night of little sleep," Erika reassured.

"Thank you, Erika. I slept quite well and have felt good so far this morning. Well enough to take a trip to Kefalonia to visit with Stefano and Anna!" she exclaimed.

"Poly kala nea!! Excellent news! I will make us some eggs and cheese for breakfast, to enjoy in the morning sunshine," and with that, she disappeared into the kitchen.

The deep burnt caramelised smell that Sophie had usually craved at least three cups of every morning, did not seem so inviting. She lifted its contents to her mouth and instantly felt the nausea rise in her stomach as she breathed in the intense coffee aroma through her nostrils, making her recoil in panic. Tipping it over the balcony and watching as the dark colour diluted into the clear salty waters, she took a few more deep breathes before taking a seat at the table. Nikolas emerged out from the doorway to join her at the table. He looked so handsome with his thick, black hair still damp from his morning shower. He pulled a chair out next to Sophie and planted a kiss on her cheek.

"You seem to radiate more beauty today, Sophie. I will have to keep you close to me on our trip, so no Greek man tries to steal your heart from me!" he exclaimed, with a smile.

"I don't think that would ever be possible. I am here for the long run," Sophie reassured him, as Erika arrived with a tray of crockery for the table.

"Kalimera, Mama!" Nikolas said, standing to give his mother a good morning kiss and to help her with the tray.

A sleepy Maria stumbled through the doorway, wrapped in a dressing gown and squinting with her half-awake eyes.

"What time are we leaving this morning, Papa?" she inquired, before even taking a seat at the table.

"The earlier, the better, matia mou!" he replied. "I have a few things to sort in Sami today, ready for the start of the season, and I need to clear out my old apartment. I still have a few things there that they need taken away, ready for the new owners," he said as Maria flopped onto the chair next to him and poured herself a glass of water.

"It's chilly out here today, even the bees have not yet returned!" Maria objected, as she wrapped her dressing gown tighter around her body and flicked the hood up over her head to keep her ears warm.

Nikolas laughed at his daughter. "You look like a warrior dressed in your robe. Are you ready to fight Helios?" he mocked.

Maria poked her tongue out at her Papa and pulled a face as Erika planted a bowl of boiled eggs on the table, accompanied by sliced cheese and bread.

Taking a seat to join them all, Erika reminded them that Lent would begin in just a week and that it would be just cheese and yoghurt through the last week of Tirini, and no further meat or dairy until after Easter.

"Make sure you fill up, Sophie, as Lent will be full of salads, greens and shellfish!" exclaimed Erika. "We have a cupboard of cheese to get through this week!"

Sophie reluctantly took an egg from the bowl and cracked open the shell, The smell made her stomach ache, but she forced a mouthful into her so Nikolas would not change his mind about her tagging along on his trip. She could feel her stomach ejecting its contents, but she refused to allow it to resurface. Taking a mouthful of water to wash it down, she reached for the safety of the bread and devoured a few slices to fill her stomach. Having remained at the table for enough time to allow the food to settle, Sophie excused herself and made her way to the safety of the bathroom.

It was just after eleven when they eventually set sail in Evangeline. Maria took ages getting herself showered and packing her suitcase in between frantically messaging her friends on social media, arranging visits and nights out in Argostoli. Hugging a farewell to Erika, who placed a €20 note in her palm, she reminded her granddaughter that she was her kardoula mou, her heart, so to keep safe whilst she was away from home.

Erika blew frantic kisses with both hands and waved them all a safe journey from the garden as Evangeline motored by. The boat skirted past the windmills at the entrance to the bay and eventually emerged into the vastness of the Ionian Sea.

It had been so long since Sophie had been on board Evangeline, and it took a short while for her to adjust to her sea legs. The nausea did not help as she battled with the motion of the sea and the urge to bend over the stern and throw up the contents of her breakfast into the waters below. Maria sat at the bow and watched as they carved through the waves sending an occasional salty spray over her. Sophie smiled as she displayed so much joy from the small droplets that stung her face like tiny shards of ice.

The water was still cold from the winter currents and did not look as inviting as it had through summer, yet the landscape of Ithaca still took Sophie's breath away. The cliffs supported a verdant carpet of spring after the amount of rainfall they had received through winter and the creaminess of the limestone rocks slated the translucent turquoise and sapphire seawater like swords from the lush vegetation above. It had seemed a lifetime since that very first visit to Ithaca with Nikolas. That had been the moment she had been seduced and mesmerised by different shades of blues and greens that could have challenged the palette of Botticelli. This tiny emerald isle seemed to arouse even the most dormant of human senses.

Skirting the coast, Sophie observed the influx of visiting sailing boats as they glided through the hidden entrance to the port of Vathy. Distinguishable only by the welcoming sight of the isolated small whitewashed chapel of Saint Andrew, blanketed by a deep green yew-covered hill and sat prominently on the rocky coast hugging the turquoise seas. An azure blue wooden door and small windows emitted a warm welcome to all those seafarers in search of a place to take rest.

The island's beauty never disappointed her. Its natural calmness seemed to lull her motion sickness as they floated by. Eventually, they neared the most southern point of the island and the first views of Sami appeared on the horizon. As they entered the Ormos Gulf, the wind picked up, and the waters became choppier, sending the boat bouncing across the waves. Sophie couldn't cope with the bobbing of the boat as it battled across the open waters, and her nausea got the best of her. She managed to reach the edge of the boat in just enough time to expel the bile that had started to build up in her mouth and was burning the back of her throat.

Nikolas felt helpless as he held onto the helm and navigated across to the open expanse of the sea towards the more sheltered bay of Agia Efimia. Sophie retched so much that nothing was now coming out of her mouth and she collapsed into a heap onto the deck of the boat, her stomach aching from the exertion. Maria passed her a bottle of water to try to remove the nasty taste from her mouth and to rehydrate her.

Nikolas glided the boat into its mooring point effortlessly, and after securing the mooring lines to the harbour wall cleat, he made his way to check on Sophie.

"It's fine, Nikolas. The motion of the boat that just took me off guard. I was absolutely fine until the wind picked up. Don't forget it's the very first time I have been on the sea for a long while, and I am not as good on my sea legs as you two!" she reminded him. "I will pop into the supermarket whilst you sort out the boat and grab something for travel sickness," she said, as Nikolas helped her to her feet.

Sophie was glad to step off the boat and feel land beneath her feet. She rejected Maria's offer to accompany her and headed towards the supermarket, still very wobbly on her legs . The feeling of nausea coming and going with the bobbing sensation still lingered. Grateful to finally reach the steps of the shop, she staggered in through the doors. Locating the toiletries section among the cramped aisles, she scanned the shelves for a pregnancy testing kit and some travel sickness tablets. Finally finding what she was looking for, she headed straight to the till to make her purchase.

She then hurried out of the shop and into the neighbouring café to use the testing kit.

Sophie felt so flustered as she sat down to use the toilet. Her heart raced as she opened the wrapper and took the cap off the tester pen. She didn't need to read the instructions. She knew exactly what to do. Sophie had been in this situation so many times previously with various boyfriends and had always been so disappointed by the final results. Excitedly, she placed the stick into her urine stream for the advised 30 seconds and placed the cap back onto the tester. Closing her eyes and remaining completely still, she turned the tester pen on its side onto her bare legs and waited for the recommended two minutes. Two minutes that seemed to take a lifetime. Her legs bounced in anticipation as she refused the temptation to check the results window and just kept a steady check on the minutes on her mobile. Time seemed to have completely stopped.

Eventually, with the two minutes up, she reluctantly turned the stick with her eyes squeezed shut, still too scared to look at the results. Prising one eye open, then the other, she finally looked at the tester pen. A smile spread across her face. Two pink lines prominently stood boldly against the lighter pink background. She was pregnant. She was only actually bloody pregnant. In the excitement of the moment, Sophie jumped up from the seat and punched the air, almost tripping over her own knickers that strapped her ankles together. Then, let out a bellowing shout of victory, without even considering what the diners inside the café might think. This was just the best news ever. She now had to think of a way to break the news gently to Nikolas.

Chapter 7

Nikolas had tied down the boat and was sat with Maria on the bench overlooking the harbour, waiting patiently for Sophie to emerge from the supermarket. With every minute that passed, he became more and more anxious about where Sophie had got to. He was just about to go in search of her just in case she had become ill when she appeared from the other side of the road.

"I am so sorry I took my time. I just needed to use the toilet. All that bobbing made my bladder so weak!" she said with a beaming smile across her face. She wanted to blurt out her news that second but knew it wasn't the right time with Maria present.

"How are you feeling now, Sophie?" questioned a concerned Nikolas.

"Amazing! I mean, I am feeling fine," she corrected, not wanting to sound too enthusiastic. "I have taken a travel sickness tablet, so I am sure my stomach will settle," she said, shaking the packet at him and lying about the medication.

"We will see. I have to do a few errands today to Sami, so we will drop Maria with Anna and spend the day together, yes?" Nikolas stated. Sophie nodded in agreement as they made their way towards Stefano's house.

Sophie had never been to Anna's house. It was set back from the main harbour and a little steep climb following a windy road towards the mountains behind the village of Agia Efimia. The walk took them about twenty minutes and was quite taxing at times, but Sophie was glad of the freshness of the day and lack of heat that would have made the walk unbearable. She was so elated with her good news that the walk could have taken an hour, and she would not have noticed one bit.

A dense hillside of Yew trees lined the pathless road on both sides, creating ample spaces between their trunks to jump out of the way of any oncoming traffic. Even the mountains were immersed in whirlwinds of colour as the different hues of greens reached to the deep blue cloudless skies above them. The wind swept the mountain floors and blew the fresh scent of wild herbs past them as they continued their gentle climb upwards. The familiar sound of clanging goat bells echoed through the trees from the mountains above.

It was not long before they took a small driveway that led them towards a newly built house nestled amongst the Yew trees. The garden was very barren and still looked very much like a building site apart from a large old olive tree that took centre of a freshly levelled patch of earth and the blue glints of a small pool that had been sunk into a freshly laid patio area to the side of the main building.

Children's bikes and toys lay discarded on the dusty floor and a familiar stern voice, scolding a crying child, could be heard coming from the rear of the property, Nikolas shouted his arrival over the shouts and sobs, then wandered through a gate to the side of the house to be greeted by a red-faced Anna, who looked absolutely exhausted.

"Yassas ,Theia Anna!" Maria said as she launched herself into Anna's arms for a hug.

"Yassas Sophie, Nikolas. It's a crazy house here today. The children are so wound up about Maria staying. They have been non-stop arguments over which room she should stay in, so be prepared for a battle Maria," warned Anna as Maria headed indoors to look for her younger cousins. "I am so glad she is finally here as I can get on with some housework. The place is a mess. Stefano has been at Sea Rock almost every day this week, getting things prepared for opening, and I am absolutely exhausted from running about after the children. I am like a nurse, cleaner, teacher, referee and cook all in one!"

"You wouldn't change it for the world, Anna!" laughed Nikolas as he gave her a kiss on both cheeks.

"Yassas, Anna!" greeted Sophie, giving her a hug.

"I must be crazy, but you are right! Are you coming in for a drink?" she motioned with her head nodding towards the kitchen.

"It's only a quick visit to drop off Maria, but could I borrow the car. My van is still parked up at Sami harbour, and I need to collect my belongings from the old house. I will bring it back later today," pleaded Nikolas.

"No problem at all, but bring it back in one piece as I know how bumpy those mountain roads are!" she smiled handing him the keys.

"Yassou Maria! Do not be trouble for Theia Anna and be careful in Argostoli. Say hello to your friends from me!" he reminded her.

"Yassou Papa! Yassou, Sophie!" came a shout in between the laughter from Maria who had disappeared somewhere inside.

Sophie said farewell to Anna and took a seat in the passenger seat of their family car. The children's car seats took over much of the rear of the ample hatchback with toys scattering both of the footwells. Sophie smiled at the thought of the abundance of baby accessories, taking over her life. Nikolas took a seat next to her, noted the radiant smile on her face and lent over to give her a kiss.

"It feels like so long since it has been just the two of us. It will be good to spend the day alone. How are your sea legs now, Sophie?" he said, playfully poking her thigh.

"I am much better now. Just a little queasy, but it's getting easier to cope with. So what is the plan for today?" she inquired.

"I need to renew my fishing licence, so I can be allowed to sell my catch to the taverna's this season and then take a few moments to collect my belongings from the old house above Sami. We shall first take lunch," he said as he turned on the ignition and headed back towards Agia Efimia and followed the coast road to Sami.

Sophie opened the window, and a burst of freshness filled the car as they pulled off the drive. Agia Efimia was so quiet as they drove the road back towards the harbour. Tourists had not yet returned to the island in hoards, and the taverna's were mostly still closed for business. There were just a few boats moored at the harbour wall, and the excursions boats were yet to return to the dock. But, in the absence of the crowds, the village emitted a dramatic contrast of indescribable beauty. A deeply historical and spiritual sleepiness that she had not experienced during her stay the previous year.

Even though the village had not been alive with "party till dawn" nightclubs or hoards of drunken teenagers on their first unescorted holiday overseas, it had still been a bustle of life with those older visitors seeking the perfect place to spend a few quiet weeks of their year. The taverna's had been packed with visitors returning to see old friends or newcomer's experiencing their first visit to this divine paradise. Holiday yachts and speedboat's had filled every gap along the harbour wall, displaying their country of origin like a meeting of nations.

They whizzed passed the churchyard on the edge of Agia Efimia, which had left a profound imprint in Sophie's soul during her previous visit. The small child's grave that had lain silently looking out to sea had made her reflect on her own life so much, take caution to the wind and led her in the direction that she had now taken. Sophie smiled fondly at the fleeting memory. Following the windy road, they skirted past the emerald hues of several hidden, inaccessible coves before reaching the outskirts of the ferry port Sami.

The streets of Sami seemed to blend classical Italian style architecture with an intoxicating Greek charm, as the village still retained the feel of an ancient market town regardless of its busy port. As they continued towards the main harbour area, the streets started to fill with people. Nikolas explained that they were mostly locals or tourists arriving from mainland Greece or Italy. Sami was the busiest seaport for Kefalonia and saw visitors all year, unlike the neighbouring Agia Efimia.

Nikolas parked up the car and suggested lunch at one of the waterside taverna's. Taking his hand, Sophie strolled in complete silence, desperate for just a perfect moment together to tell him their unexpected news. Nikolas pulled her close and wrapped his arm around her waist as they followed the promenade next to the deep blueness of the Ionian Sea. A few shoals of small fish were enjoying the sunrays that penetrated the water surface, illuminating the depths below.

A distinguished gentleman, wearing a welcoming smile, came out of one of the waterside taverna's to greet Nikolas as they passed by. Frantically shaking his hand like a long lost friend, he introduced himself to Sophie as Dimitri and planted a double kiss to each of her cheeks. Sophie observed this charismatic character that seemed to radiate happiness. His grey receding hairline was combed back from his forehead. A set of spectacles hung over his blue shirt that was casually opened from the neck, exposing just a few escaping chest hairs. After a quick chat with Nikolas, he extended his arm to invite them into his taverna.

A handsome young waiter with piercing blue eyes and a thick head of black curly hair greeted them both and showed them to their seats. He pulled out two chairs from under a table that overlooked the lapping water and gave incredible views back towards Agia Efimia. Taking a seat, he offered Sophie a menu and took out his note pad, requesting their order for drinks.

"A cold Mythos beer for me and a coffee for you, Sophie?" Nikolas questioned.

"Just water for me, parakalo!' Sophie replied, not wanting anything that might restart the nausea, after her morning experience.

And with a slight nod, the waiter disappeared across the road to the main building to get their drinks.

"Nikolas! How are you? You have been away for so long!" came a bubbly melodic female voice from behind them. A lady in her late fifties, approached the table. A thick head of auburn hair reached to her shoulders slightly greying at the roots and her smiling brown eyes that twinkled as she spoke. She grabbed Nikolas by his shoulders and pulled him into a friendly kiss.

"Yassas Kiki!! You are looking so beautiful as always," he teased. "How has Dimitri not tired you out just yet? Kiki, this is Sophie. She moved from England to be here with me, can you believe!" he exclaimed, reaching for Sophie's hand.

"Welcome to Sami and Dolphins Restaurant, my dear. You radiate beauty, and Nikolas is lucky to have you by his side. If you were here alone, you would be snapped up in no time!" she smiled. "I keep Dimitri calm and will not take any of his tantrums. I am in the kitchen, and he is out here, so we don't get in each other's way. This is how we have lasted together so long. He is getting a little grumpier with age, but don't tell him I said this!" she laughed.

"It is good to meet you, Kiki" Sophie smiled back politely.

"How is you Mama, Nikolas? I have not seen her on the island for a long time. Tell her to call me as I would like to speak with her again," Kiki continued. She remained with them for a few moments before the waiter returned with drinks and to take their food order.

Kiki was a bubbly character with a very calm and relaxed personality. She was pretty quick-witted and had Sophie laughing with her sharp remarks during their short encounter. Leaving them to place their orders, Kiki disappeared across the road and into the main building.

"Dimitri and Kiki have been family friends for a long time, and both knew my Papa very well. They are like family to me. They have had this taverna now for almost 30 years. I would visit here with Papa after a trip at sea for a good seafood meze without Mama knowing. That was before he disappeared at sea. Dimitri organised a search around a cluster of remote islands, a little south of Zakynthos, where his distress flare had been seen. But they found nothing. We had a family meal here for his memory. So it holds a special place in my heart," Nikolas explained. "Now, what would you like to eat Sophie?"

Chapter 8

Having finished an incredible seafood lunch, Nikolas had left
Sophie at Dolphin's Restaurant momentarily and headed to the
port office to complete his paperwork to renew his fishing licence.
With his forms completed and fee paid in full, he made his way
back to the taverna. The spring sunshine was warm and Nikolas
did not feel the need for them to rush around. They needed some
quality time together before heading back to Ithaca. He had not
yet shown her Karavomylos Lake, and this would be a great day to
see it in the peacefulness of early spring without too many
tourists. He remembered how much he loved to see the wonder
of Sophie's face when he took her somewhere for the first time.

Nikolas re-joined Sophie who was happily watching the boats
coming and going as she sipped at a glass of cold iced water.
Suggesting a walk before heading to the mountains above Sami,
they strolled along the seafront until they had left the built-up
port area behind reached a green break in the landscape. This
followed a road that ran alongside a long stretch of pebbly beach
skirted by a few large houses hidden from view in amongst large
Eucalyptus trees. It eventually led them to the small village of
Karavomylos. Passing by two large hotels, a small quay with a
handful of boats and a sports stadium that had the most
impressive views across the ocean, they came to a lake hidden by
trees in the most spectacular location.

With its open ocean views and a backdrop of lush green
vegetation, a glimmer of a church spire and the abundance of
wildfowl on the water, it seemed to create such a magical
atmosphere. This had to be the prettiest seaside trail that Sophie
had ever walked. As they followed the cobbled path around the
lake, incredible views towards Ithaca filled the vista on the
horizon. Nikolas explained that, just like Melissani Lake, the
waters at Karavomylos were part of the same strange phenomena.
Here, the water also traversed underground from the Katavorthes,
on the western side of the island. It had miraculously emerged
here after finding its way up through the cracks in the rock,

caused by the islands many earthquakes. Sophie was listening but her mind was not really focused on what Nikolas had told her and she felt herself distancing from the moment.

In the far corner, under the shade of a cluster of Eucalyptus trees, was a pretty taverna providing sea views to one-side and lake views to another. Sophie suggested that they could take a rest under the trees and have a quick drink before continuing to his old home. This, she felt, would be the most perfect place to tell Nikolas their news. Taking a seat close to the water allowing her to take in the beauty and serenity of the landscape, her heart raced as Nikolas disappeared to order their drinks. She felt sick at the thought of telling him. They had not really been together that long, and for most of her time on these Ionian islands, Nikolas had been on the mainland. They had never even spoken about having a family together. What if he didn't want another child. What if he went crazy, and they ended up breaking up. How would she cope as a single mother alone, miles away from her family?

For a few moment's she argued with her own conscience. One minute deciding against telling him the news, then deciding she had to tell him because he might actually be excited. Her mind battled with what to do as Nikolas returned to the table and handed Sophie another glass of iced water.

"Sophie, is everything OK today? You seem too away with the birds and not really here. You are not even drinking the vast quantity of coffee that you have usually filled up on before lunch!' he said observantly.

Sophie did have an addiction to coffee and needed numerous cups a day to function correctly. This had been something that she had always had an issue with. It had kept her awake on multiple occasions and found her surfing so many dodgy internet sites, making totally random buys from QVC or watching dated repeats from the '90s on Comedy classics as the caffeine bounced unstoppably around her system. Even after trying to go caffeine-free, she failed miserably after reverting back to her old habit after just three days clean and continually feeling like a zombie.

Plucking up courage, she opened her mouth to tell Nikolas what was on her mind, but the words would not come out. Instead, she managed a shrug and smiled at him as she took a mouthful of water to quench her dry mouth. Sophie was mad at herself for chickening out and absorbed her attention towards a few ducks that had swum over in the hope of a few bread crusts to snack on.

"I know there is something not right, Sophie. You are just to quiet, plus your eyes are not sparkling like a child's like they usually do when I bring you somewhere different," he continued. "If I have done something to upset you, then you must tell me so I can understand and make it better for us!" he stated in a concerned manner.

"You have not done anything that could ever upset me, Nikolas. Everything is just perfect. It always is. That's what bothers me the most. What if something happened accidentally to make it not so perfect? What if I did something that upset you?" Sophie questioned.

Nikolas looked at her, bewildered by what she was saying. "I do not understand, Sophie. How can anything be too perfect? What could you do to upset me? Look at everything you have done to make me the happiest man in all of Greece. Without you becoming my wife, I could not be happier!" he exclaimed.

"What if I became pregnant? What if I was carrying your child" she questioned, hoping he would give her some idea how it would make him feel.

"If you were carrying my child, I would be so honoured and tell the Gods from the top of Mount Ainos the incredible news. Is that what is bothering you? Are you pregnant, Sophie?" he questioned.

61

Sophie looked at Nikolas and nodded her head. Without any warning, Nikolas jumped out of his seat and lifted Sophie out of her chair. He held her tightly as her feet left the ground, and he swung her around in his arms. Tears ran down his face as he hugged her with his strong arms. He kept muttering out loudly in Greek, none of which Sophie could understand. Eventually, Nikolas calmed down and placed both hands on Sophie's stomach.

"How long have you known Sophie? How long do we have until we are parents? We need to have you checked to see if everything is OK," Nikolas said, in a fluster from the news.

"I have only found out this morning. That is why I came with you and Maria. I needed a pregnancy test just in case I had got it wrong. That is why I was feeling sick and lightheaded. And why I have been getting fatter and not because of Erika's rovani!" she added.

"I am so happy right now, I could burst!" Nikolas said, wiping the tears from his face. "I promise I will not let anything happen to you or our baby. We will move to Kefalonia, so we are close to the hospital. I will not risk losing you Sophie!"

"It is too early to worry about the birth yet, Nikolas. We need to have the pregnancy confirmed by a doctor to find out how many weeks I am and when the baby is due. Then we can make a plan," Sophie said in a calming tone.

"We will visit with the doctor here in Sami today. They will be able to tell us everything we need to know," Nikolas replied, taking Sophie by the hand. "Come, let us visit with them now and see if they have an appointment for us."

Sophie had never seen Nikolas so excited. He had acted in a way she had not expected but had really hoped for. The smile did not leave his face as he almost dragged her all the way to the medical centre, stopping only a few times to check that Sophie was OK. Having briefly spoken to the medical staff at the counter regarding her situation, Sophie took a seat in the waiting room and left Nikolas chatting with the receptionist. After a while of what seemed like a negotiation with the medical staff, Nikolas eventually re-joined her. He advised he had managed to get an appointment for her to be seen as a matter of urgency. He handed her a few forms that she needed to fill in so that she could be registered with a doctor, and they could examine her as she was not yet a Greek citizen.

Sophie felt anxious about the wait. She really wanted the test to be accurate. It was such an unexpected but welcome surprise and one that she had most definitely not planned. She remembered how Erika had teased her over Christmas as she had made the Christopsomo bread and had hoped that the New year would bring a new baby. This was her doing Sophie thought. Erika had wished this upon them, and for that, she felt so grateful. This was Sophie's first real chance of being a mother after all other attempts in the past had come back negative, and she would do anything for her home test to be accurate.

A nurse called Sophie's name, and, with Nikolas by her side, she followed her to the consultancy room. After a gentle examination of Sophie's abdomen, a quick chat about dates and handing over a specimen of her urine, the doctor confirmed a positive result. Nikolas became a blubbering mess again as they gave an expected due date in September. Having completed all the necessary forms and registering her details, they left the centre, both radiating with joy.

Nikolas spent the remainder of the day touching and kissing Sophie's stomach, telling anyone who walked past their good news and checking that Sophie was feeling okay. Having travelled up to the old house above Sami to collect the remainder of his possessions, Nikolas handed the keys for the house to the estate agents and they made their way back towards Agia Efimia to drop off the car to Stefano and Anna. Deciding against breaking the news and keeping it secret for just a few more weeks until the pregnancy made it to the twelve week scan and the threat of a miscarriage had passed.

It was going to be so hard to stop Nikolas from shouting the news from the mountaintop, as he had suggested. She had never seen him so happy, not since she had returned back to Kefalonia after their brief holiday romance. It would also be difficult for Sophie not to tell her parents the good news as they had given up hope of ever becoming grandparents. She was also desperate to tell her best friend Amy, who at that moment was halfway up Kilimanjaro, raising money in aid of Greenpeace. The news would rock Amy's world as she had always wanted to become an unofficial Auntie as she had pledged never to have children of her own when there were enough orphans to consider adopting without stretching and disfiguring her own lady bits.

The boat trip back to Ithaca seemed even more magical as the reality of the pregnancy began to sink in. This was to become the very island where she would become a mother and raise her own child next to the man that she loved so passionately. How things could change so quickly. In less than a year she had been jilted at the alter, honeymooned alone, moved countries to chase after a man she had known just a few weeks, been thrust into a culture and religion she knew nothing about, found her dream home and now, to top it all off, had found out she was pregnant with Nikolas' child. She would have laughed if anyone had told her a year ago that this was her future. It was almost as if her childhood dreams that she had almost given up on were starting to come true. Nothing could make it anymore perfect.

Chapter 9

The next few weeks were so exciting for Sophie and Nikolas as they kept their secret from everyone. Sophie spent some time shopping in Argostoli for baby items and hidden them away at Villa Elysian. She was still very reluctant to become to excited until after the 12 week scan when she could relax a little more and enjoy the pregnancy. Morning sickness was now becoming harder to hide as almost everything that Erika cooked turned her stomach and she could not face coffee at all. Her baby belly had started to protrude slightly which she hid well under baggy clothes.

Early April brought Easter celebrations to all of Greece. Erika busied herself with the old traditions and changed her wardrobe from winter to summer clothes, she changed the furnishings to a more vibrant summer pattern, given the entire house a thorough clean and spent hours in the garden making it burst with colour. Erika and Nikolas both joined in the daily church services in the little church above the village. Erika flooded the house with the sweet and yeasty warm aroma of baked Tsoureki, the traditional Easter bread. She taught Sophie how to decorate eggs with leaves, boiling them in red dye, leaving an imprint of the leaf on the shell and filling a basket with the pretty results.

Wafts of caramelised brown sugar, spicy cinnamon and vanilla tickled her appetite as soft moist cookies straight from the oven, cooled on the baking rack just minutes from their crunchy perfection all ready for the children who would visit the house over the Easter weekend. Sophie accompanied Nikolas at the Resurrection of Christ midnight vigil to experience the importance of this custom to the villagers. Holding lit candles, they sang hymns and listened to the priests' sermon followed by the ringing of the church bells and a display of fireworks that shot a rainbow of sparkles over the bay.

Easter Sunday arrived with the blessing of warm spring sunshine and a fresh sea breeze. It also symbolised the end of Lent, and the welcomed return of meat to the menu. The aroma of sweet lamb, rolled in fresh sprigs of rosemary, being cooked on a spit over an open fire, filled almost all the garden's of Kioni. Jenny and George at the Spavento bar, had a whole lamb roasting over a sizeable old charcoal filled oil drum barbeque set up close to the watersedge. They plated the meat along with an array of salads, cheese eggs and bread, ready to share with anyone who wandered over to join them ahead of their own family Easter celebrations.

Taking a wander to the village, they were welcomed by Aleka, Panos and Yiorgos from the mini market and Taso from the nearby Agnandio Villa apartments. Sophie had been a little overwhelmed by the celebrations and, even though she was not religious, had full respect for the customs and traditions that she had chosen to become apart of. After filling their stomachs for a second time that day with their own spit-roasted feast, together with kokoretsi, a fully satisfied Sophie had retired early for a much-needed nap.

April had also brought with it a little less rain and a bit more warmth, plus the days had started to lengthen. The daisies, poppies and cyclamens were beginning to blossom, sending a carpet of colour across the landscape. This also meant that the air was once again filled with the scent of wildflowers and herbs that intoxicated the breeze as they sat outdoors under the almost cloudless skies. The familiar sound of goat bells could now be heard closer to the village as they returned to the pastures to feed off the fresh spring shoots that sprouted from the grasses above Philoxenia. Birds had started to build their nests and chirped away frantically as if in constant singing contest in the hope of attracting a mate.

The yachts had also started to return to Kioni harbour, bringing a steady influx of nautical enthusiasts to the village and boosting the income of the local tavernas and shops as they filled up with goods ready for their seafaring adventures. As they sat on the veranda at Philoxenia and watched the yachts drift by, Sophie mentioned to Nikolas the thought of sailing into the wind together was rather old style romantic, and, as she had never actually been on a yacht, she would love to do the island hopping thing one day.

Villa Elysian was now ready for them to move into and, after they had said their thank you'd and farewell's to Erika, they spent their first official night in their new home. Sophie settled into life at the villa almost immediately and loved the fresh views of the island that gifted her eyes every morning. Rural mountain life in Exhogi was a little different to the calming coastal life of Kioni. Here the air was a little chillier and the scents so different to the salty essence of the sea she had been accustomed to. The mountains were filled with wild herbs that crunched underfoot with the early morning frost sending a fresh burst of aromatics upwards into the air as she took her breakfast on the veranda. Herds of mountain goats roamed the surrounding scrubland, surprising Sophie with their sudden bleats and serenading her with the soft clanking of their goat bells as they gently grazed the mountain floor.

Shopping was also a much different experience. Bread was delivered by the local bread van and left in a bag hanging from the gate that Sophie would leave filled with money, ready for his arrival. Milk and Eggs were bought from a small shop in Exhogi whilst fruit and vegetables were delivered by a truck that would wander the mountain villages selling his produce straight from the boats that arrived in Vathy from the neighbouring islands of Lefkada and Kephalonia. Sophie saw it as a primitive version of Tesco home delivery services that she had used regularly back in the UK. It also meant that she did not have to worry about travelling to Vathy just to get the essentials.

A week after settling into Villa Elysian. Sophie received her letter to confirm her twelve-week scan and was now itching to share their secret with the rest of the family. Her bump was starting to become hard to conceal as her clothes became a little tighter, but, being at Villa Elysian had made things a little easier. The morning sickness had subsided, but she had obtained an unhealthy craving for cheese that she devoured at any given opportunity.

The day of the scan arrived and after travelling to Sami in Evangeline, they headed to Argostoli. Sophie had radiated with excitement as they walked the white sterile corridors of the hospital. Announcing their arrival, they both anxiously took a seat in the waiting room. The room was filled with young mothers cradling large bumps, excited first time parents-to-be gripping each others hands and young toddlers throwing around toys from the donated toy box as their tired pregnant mother looked on. The room was overbearingly warm and the wait seemed to take much longer than they had anticipated. Sophie had drunk so much water that she was almost at the point of creating a puddle on the floor beneath her seat as they were eventually called into the consultancy room.

Laying on the bed, Sophie lowered her trousers just enough to expose the rapidly growing bump. The sonographer rubbed a cold gel over Sophie's abdomen and reassured her that the pressure might cause some discomfort. Turning to smile at Nikolas, Sophie grabbed his hand for reassurance. The sonographer remained in silence as she rubbed the device over her stomach, pressing a little too hard against her bladder making her leak uncontrollably for a split second. It seemed to take ages, which made Sophie slightly anxious.

Just as Sophie feared the worst, the consultant turned the screen to show a clear image of a perfectly formed foetus curled up inside her with its heartbeat pumping away frantically in its tiny chest. Sophie could not contain her joy and burst into tears, as the moment was just so precious. Nikolas kissed her hand tenderly and smiled at the images on the screen. Leaving the room they beamed with joy as they held the scan images of their unborn child. Making a desperate exit, Sophie just managed to make it to the toilet to relieve herself without embarrassment, leaving Nikolas stood alone with his thoughts.

Nikolas beamed uncontrollably as he looked at the perfect scan photos of his tiny baby in his hand. He had never even considered becoming a father again. The whole pregnancy had taken him by surprise, but he was overjoyed at the idea of having another child with Sophie. Seeing his baby inside her made him fiercely protective. He felt the fear of his past rise up inside him. He would never let anything happen to Sophie. He would not let her down as he had his Evangeline. He wanted Sophie to share the rest of his life alongside him as he had so many adventures planned for them both. Now those adventures would include their child. Tears ran down his face as he felt his emotions well up inside him. He could not wait to share the news with Maria and Erika. He could not begin to tell Sophie how much he loved her for giving him this incredible gift. He would make sure that nothing would ever harm his little bubble of happiness. He knew what he needed to do to make this even more perfect. To make them the family Sophie had dreamed of since a child.

Sophie wandered towards Nikolas, who was stood staring at the scan photographs and had not even noticed her approaching.

"Hey Papa!" she said, placing her hand on his shoulder. "It's incredible, isn't it? Our child is so perfect already and happily resting inside here," she said, prodding her now emptied abdomen.

"I am blown away with it all, Sophie. I do not think I could be any happier at this moment. You do know how much I love you, don't you?" he questioned.

"What's got into you. Of course, I know. Let's get back and break the news to everyone!" she said excitedly.

"I have a better idea! Let me just make a call, and I might have a surprise for us to share tonight. We can keep a secret for just another day. Let us enjoy it for ourselves for this moment," and with that, Nikolas kissed her cheek and disappeared ahead of her with his mobile pressed to his ear.

Sophie was left baffled by his behaviour. What was he up to? She thought as she slowly followed behind him. She had no clue what

69

he was arranging as she listened to him chattering away in Greek on his mobile phone. After saying his goodbyes, he turned and smiled at Sophie.

"Come, I have the best night planned for us both. You will really love where we are going," reaching for her hand, he led her to his van.

"Where are we going, Nikolas! Tell me!" Sophie begged as they left Argostoli and headed into the mountains and towards Assos.

"My mouth is sealed until we get there!" he stated, playfully mimicking a zip closing across his lips.

Sophie sat back, defeated in the passenger seat and felt herself drift off deep into her own thoughts. Her mind was filled with images of their future together as a family. A baby that would be so precious to them both. As she pondered through the various baby names that she had always liked over the years, none of them seemed relevant to her now. She wondered what Nikolas would want to call their daughter or son?

Her eyes scanned the breath-taking scenery of the dramatic coastline as it floated by. The sheer cliffs that dropped away into the depths of the ocean below were endless on the horizon. They seemed to follow the isolated coast road for a considerable amount of time, without any signs of civilisation, apart from the occasional vacant mountain holiday home. She was now famished as it was after lunch, and, with Nikolas still refusing to tell her where they were heading, she tried her best to pick up their route on Google maps, but with no signal, she failed miserably.

Eventually, they passed a sign for Myrtos and Assos, making Sophie think they might be heading for his uncle's restaurant in Fiscardo or a visit to the beach in Assos, where she nearly drowned. But that would not be somewhere she wanted to return to in a hurry.

After passing by the spectacular white sands of Myrtos beach, Nikolas indicated to turn onto a gated driveway with "Villa Nel Cielo" on a stone sign. Pressing a sequence of numbers onto the electronic pad on one of the stone pillar's, the gates slowly opened to reveal an imposing villa painted in a light eggshell and khaki colour that looked reminiscent of a 1970s block of flats. The van came to a halt as the gates closed behind them. Sophie stepped out onto the driveway, confused by their location.

"Nikolas, where are we? Why are we here?" she questioned as Nikolas eventually appeared from inside the car.

"My Sophie, this will take your breath away more than my face in the morning!" he teased.

Chapter 10

Nikolas took Sophie by the hand and led her through the front door of the villa. The smell of spices and herbs being cooked wafted through the air and made Sophie's stomach rumble out loudly. A gentleman wearing a waiter's uniform greeted them. He led them past a contemporary open plan kitchen, that would have been perfectly suitable for any high class restaurant, where a chef was busy preparing food in front of a traditional wood-fired oven. The living room was just as incredible and designed around a central fireplace surrounded by exquisite, vibrant ethnic printed fabric that stood out from the slate grey of the walls and floor. A wolf skin rug lay on the floor in front of the open log fire that crackled as the flames leapt and danced in the grate.

Leading them through a sliding glass door, they stepped onto an elegant seating area set between a few imposing concrete pillars that held up the balcony above. Below them was a larger patio with a comfy seating area with invitingly colourful scatter cushions that looked out over the uninterrupted ocean views. The waiter extended his arm to a table that was perfectly laid ready for a fine dining experience. He then disappeared back inside and left them alone to explore.

Sophie could not take in the immense beauty that surrounded them. They appeared to be perched on the edge of a cliff that floated above the ocean. To her left, Sophie could see the perfection of Myrtos beach in its full dreamy extent a few hundred yards below them and the endless vistas of the white limestone cliffs that stretched to the West that they had driven just minutes before. To her right, she could make out the ruined Venetian castle that sat overlooking the enchanting bay of Assos that she had once visited with Nikolas. To the front of her, a cylindrical fire pit sat in the centre of the semi circular patio reaching out to an Aztec style infinity plunge pool, hovering over the ocean and seemed to offer any bathers a chance to touch the clouds as they looked out over the endless horizon. From every angle she looked the views were sensational.

"Wow. Just Wow. This place is insane. I thought our villa had the best views, but this takes some beating! Who owns this place?" Sophie said, still taking in the magnitude of the landscape and gardens around her.

"It is the most magnificent villa in all of Kefalonia and owned by a good friend, Nicolas and Marina, his wife. They bought it as a long time ago and spent many years transforming it from a tiny square house to this amazing home you stand in now. They live in Switzerland most of the year and only stay here in the summer months. The rest of the time, it is rented out to those who can afford to stay. I called Nicolas and ask if I could use it for us to celebrate our news, just for one night." he explained. "You told me once that you would like to see the sunset on Myrtos beach, so that is what we will do tonight after we have eaten."

"You really are the most amazing man, Nikolas. This is simply the most incredibly romantic thing anyone has ever done for me. How did I end up with someone as perfect as you?" she said as she wandered over and gave him a kiss, just as the waiter returned to announce that food would be served within the hour.

Requesting a bottle of chilled sparkling water for Sophie and a Mythos beer for himself, Nikolas took Sophie's hand and guided her down a pathway below the pool. It led them through a plethora of oregano, sage and thyme that rubbed against her, releasing their pungent earthy aromas into the air as they made their way down a few cobbled steps to a secluded seating area. Three throne-like stone chairs looked out towards the horizon as if waiting for Poseidon himself to emerge from the waters below, take a seat and watch the mesmerising hues of the sunset with an ouzo in one hand and his pitchfork in another.

"There is more, Sophie, This is where we shall watch as the sun goes down,' he continued, as he led her to a pretty stone shepherds hut with a green wooden slated roof that was completely engulfed by nature. Inside was a day bed perfect for

73

relaxing as the waves crashed against the rocks below and the sun sank over the watery horizon.

Nikolas continued to take her on a tour of the villa, including the impressive master bedroom on the upper floor with its contemporary fireplace and private terrace. Then the separate one bedroomed guesthouse, immaculately furnished in the same elegant and chic style. Sophie had never been in a property designed to such perfection, even embracing the colours of the landscape that it was built on. This is how her rich Hollywood idols must have lived, she thought, as she sat down in the garden with her fluted glass of chilled sparkling water.

Their meal was as divine as the house, having been served a meal fit for the Gods. Feeling so full and content after finishing up the final mouthful of the creamy goat's cheese from the platter she had been served, Sophie sunk back into the scatter cushions, pulled her trousers down to expose her skin and patted her belly gently.

"I hope you liked your meal, little one!" she said, rubbing her stomach tenderly.

"I still am finding this so crazy, Sophie. How things can change so quickly. This time last year, I was out on the oceans and feeling very alone. Maria had left after an Easter break, and my heart was so empty. I spent all my time busy, so I did not think about my empty bed. Now look at us. I would not have been able to wish this to be true as I could never believe my life would be this way again!" Nikolas said, leaning forward and kissing her exposed bump.

As the sun started to sink into the evening sky, the views over the ocean were as incredible as Sophie had imagined. Clutching a chilled bottle of water and champagne from the fridge along with two glasses into his chest, Nikolas led Sophie back down towards the stone thrones and set the contents of his arms down on the stone table. Lighting the small fire pit, Nikolas grabbed a blanket from the shepherd's hut and placed it over their legs as he took a seat on the soft cushions next to her. Wrapping his arms around her shoulders, he pulled her into his chest as the sun started to perform its evening show.

The sky illuminated as if it was on fire in a way that Sophie had only dreamt. She never had in her life watched the sunset from such a mind-blowing location. She felt as if she was on top of the world and could never get any higher as the horizon changed from gold's to magenta and then to the deepest violet. The deep blue of the night arrived with only the twinkling of stars filling the sky above them. Nikolas raised himself from the chair to pour a small glass of champagne for Sophie and a full drink for himself. Turning to look at Sophie, as the warm glow of the fire danced on her skin, he had not felt such a rush of pure love fill his veins in such a long time.

Their eyes connected, and nothing could break their gaze. Sophie felt her heartbeat faster with so much desire as she stared back at the man that had stolen her heart and sanity. Without a single word spoken, Nikolas dropped to his knee in front of her and reached for her hand.

"Sophie, I know today could not get any crazier, but I know that you are my destiny. I know that I could never be happy again without you by my side. I have not really planned this very well as it has been pretty impulsive, but I want to ask you if you would honour me by being my wife. Will you marry me, Sophie?" he said in the most sincere voice she had heard.

Sophie had not seen this coming and, with the amount of happiness already flowing through her veins, did not even believe it would be possible to be any happier than she had been already that day. She didn't need to think about her answer as this was the most natural reply that she would ever give.

"Yes, Nikolas! Yes!! I would be so honoured to be your wife!" she replied, immediately launching herself into his arms as she saw the whiteness of his teeth burst into a massive grin across his face.

"I am the happiest man alive today!!!!" he shouted towards the heavens before pulling her deeper into an embrace. " I have not bought you any ring just yet as I did not really make good plans, but we will design one together from the jeweller in Kioni. I cannot believe how happy my heart is today. We will arrange our marriage before the baby arrives, Yes?" Nikolas said eagerly. Carefully scooping her up in his arms, he carried her into the hideaway, lay her on the bed and shut out the chill of the April night sky.

Chapter 11

Sophie woke the next morning and opened the glass doors of the master suite at Villa Nel Cielo. The clouds were thick and covered the landscape below, making her feel like she had woken up high above Earth in a temple meant only for the divine. Just a few of the mountain peaks along the coast to Assos could be seen poking through the white carpet that suffocated the dramatic vistas that her vision had feasted on the day previous. The warm wisps of steam from the small infinity pool seemed to be sucked into the atmosphere and became part of the surrounding cloudscape.

Sophie felt an urge to sink herself into the water and bath above the clouds, like a Greek Goddess. Finding her way onto the patio below, she checked that they were alone before dropping her dressing gown to the floor, exposing her full nakedness and stepped into the plunge pool. She felt as if she was offering herself to the God's as she sunk her voluptuous body under the warm waters, submersing herself from the morning chill blowing down from the mountains behind. This all felt so surreal. She felt as though she was in the most fantastic dream that she didn't want to wake up from.

Nikolas woke and reached out for Sophie to pull her into a hug, only to feel an empty coldness in her place. He took a few minutes to come around before wandering out onto the balcony to see where she had got to. Looking downwards, he could see her peacefully enjoying the warmth of the pool as she looked out over the clouds that had created a magical backdrop in contrast to the clarity of the day previous. Taking his mobile from his hand, he captured the perfection of this tranquil moment with Sophie's peachy cheekiness in full view. How he adored every inch of this beautiful woman who was now carrying his child and soon to be his wife.

Wandering downstairs, he slipped out of his boxers and stepped into the pool to join her.

"Kalimino, Mrs. Manolatos!" he said contently as he pulled her into his body and caressed her shoulder.

"Good morning Husband to be!" she replied with a smile and enjoying the feel of his slippery naked skin against hers. "I feel as though I am floating with sheer happiness above the rest of the world,' she continued in her dreamy state.

Nikolas smiled as he looked out over the bellows of clouds that drifted dreamily below them.

"We will take breakfast and head back early this morning as I cannot wait to share our news with Mama. We have so much to plan, Sophie!" he said, splashing the water playful over her face.

"Yes, we do, we really do!" she said, pushing him by the shoulders under the water.

Having taken a light breakfast on the veranda as the clouds had disbursed gifting them with one last view of the surrounding landscape, they headed back to the port of Sami. Navigating Evangeline over the clear waters of the Ionian seas and back towards the island of Ithaca, Sophie let the warmth of the morning sunshine kiss her cheeks as Nikolas carved the seas ahead.

The slow return of summer was now teasing them as they reached the end of April and headed into May. They had spent the previous night discussing their Wedding, deciding to marry ahead of the birth and agreeing on June as Nikolas had explained it was considered to be a lucky month being named after Hera, the Greek goddess of marriage. Sophie was reaching almost five months of pregnancy and could feel her body glowing with the changes it was experiencing.

As they skirted the coastline, Sophie allowed the beauty of the Ithaca to sink into her deeper. Kioni still took her breath away the moment they entered the bay passing the three dormant windmill ruins that stood like protective giants at the secluded entrance.

The picturesque village sat sleepily at the foot of the lushness of the vegetation behind as the turquoise waters of the bay lapped gently at its shallows. This whole island had a magic that had seemed to bewitch her mind and its calming atmosphere relaxed her whole body the moment she returned.

As they appeared through the inlet, Sophie noted Erika sat in her usual spot in the garden of Philoxenia drinking from a mug with her trusty ginger cat laying across her lap, soaking up the warm morning sunrays. Seeing Evangeline drift by, Erika jumped up from her seat in excitement and frantically waved across the water sending the startled cat crashing to the ground for the hundredth time. Sophie found this process so comical as she could not understand why the cat chose to sit on Erika's lap knowing that he would possibly end up suddenly ejected from his comfort.

Having moored Evangeline, they made their way along the windy road to Philoxenia. Sophie held onto Nikolas hand so tightly as the excitement filled her body. Keeping the pregnancy a secret from everyone had been so difficult and she was now desperate to share their secret with everyone. As the arrived, Erika was already at the garden gate ready to greet them both. Sophie looked around the familiar gardens had started to burst with life as the season had begun to change and the sun had started to warm the soil. Picking a woody sprig of Rosemary from the bush as she wandered by, Sophie took a deep breath of its fresh slightly lavender-like perfume and gave a smile as her mind regressed just for a second.

"It is so good to have you both back at Philoxenia. It has been far to quiet on my own after having company for so long. I have been going crazy without my family to cook for. Come, I have the kettle on to make us a fresh pot of coffee," she said, pulling both Sophie and Nikolas in for a kiss.

Taking a seat on the veranda, Nikolas and Sophie were like excitable children as they waited for Erika to join them at the table. She seemed to take forever in the kitchen as she fussed about creating them with the perfect mid-morning snack of cheese and bread. Nikolas became a little impatient and went inside to help her with the preparations, just to speed her along.

"Slow down Nikolas! What has got into you? You are like the cold winter wind over the Ionian seas with your unwelcome rush!" Erika objected.

Eventually, having settled at the table and spent a little time telling her about their evening at Villa Cel Neilo, Nikolas could not wait any longer

"Mama, we have some news for you that I know will make your heart sing," he began "I asked Sophie to be my wife and she has accepted. We will be married in June if we can get it arranged quick enough," he smiled, waiting for her reaction.

Erika jumped up from the table, her hands covered her mouth as she searched for the words to say before extending her arms and reaching for Sophie from across the table.

"This is the best news. Welcome to our family Sophie. You will really be like another daughter for me now, like Anna. It will be such an honour for you to share our name! Manolatos is a good strong name that tells we once came from the mainland" she said, kissing her cheeks from side to side. "I will get us a stronger drink so we can celebrate. Coffee is not really for this kind of news!" And she stood up to retreat indoors.

"Mama, there is something else we have to tell you!" Nikolas said reaching for her arm to stop her from leaving the table. "Sophie is pregnant and will be having my child. You will be a Yiayia again in September if all goes well!" he announced grinning from ear to ear.

Erika fell back in her chair and tears ran uncontrollably down her face.

"Mama Mia!! This is all so much to take in. I don't know what to say. I am so pleased for you both. Sophie, you will make the best Mama!" she cried. "A wedding and a new baby in the next few months! This year will be filled with good fortune. I will have lots to do. Lots of baking. Nikolas I am so happy," she said, reaching inside the cup of her bra and pulling out a scrunched up tissue to wipe away her tears.

"I will get the whiskey anyway so I can toast to your good health!" Erika smiled, as she wandered into the kitchen, with any excuse for an early morning tipple.

They chatted with an excited Erika about their plans for a few delicious hours in the morning sunshine overlooked by just the lulling sea and the sound of the singing birds. Sophie could not believe that by the end of the coming year she would be a wife and a mother, just like her childhood dreams. Yet the paradise setting of this sleepy Greek island, far surpassed everything that she had ever dreamed of as a child.

Sophie spent the afternoon on Face time, breaking their news and sharing her growing bump with her excited parents who were thrilled with the announcement that they were to become grandparents at last after giving up on the prospect many years previous. After the initial shock of the expense of yet another Wedding to arrange within a year of her being jilted by James, they seemed happy about their daughters news. It also gave them the perfect excuse to finally visit Kefalonia and Ithaca plus meet the man who had stolen their daughter's heart in a whirlwind. Sophie sent a picture of the scan to her mother who had instantly become a blubbering mess and could not wait to share the news with her friends at the local Bingo hall.

Sophie tried several times to get in contact with Amy, who was still travelling around India and consistently unavailable. When she did eventually get through it had been like trying to communicate with a darlek and she had not even known if Amy had heard her double whammy news. Getting fed up with the

81

constant "Can you hear me?" and "Your breaking up!", she gave up completely and ended up sending a text message in hope that her best friend would call her back.

The contractors turned to complete the pool just as the heat started to rise through May creating a building site in the garden plus a constant run of coffee's to keep them happy as they worked. Sophie watched over their work under the shade of the grapevine whilst completely submersed in wedding research and potential wedding venue's for their ceremony. Having eventually decided on Lazaretto island, Sophie contacted a local Wedding planner to assist in arranging the celebrations. She had set her heart on having the ceremony there as it would remind her so much of her very first visit to the island.

Nikolas returned to the seas, and set off every morning with the break of dawn to sell his catch to the islands taverna's. He had taken a few shifts at the Sea Rock restaurant in Agia Efimia with his brother, Stefano, to make money for the Wedding and arrival of the baby. Sophie also joined them for a few shifts, against Nikolas wishes. She loved returning to where she had first set eyes on these incredible islands and where everything had first started. The bustle of tourism had now arrived back on the island and created a completely different atmosphere to the once deserted resort. Sophie enjoyed chatting with the tourists about their visit, giving them a few attractions to add to their schedules and reciting the mythological stories of Odysseus and Homer that Nikolas had once shared with her. With Anna joining them, they made the perfect family team, working the restaurant in complete unison and knowing exactly when to help each other out like a silent sixth sense.

After one of her evening shifts, Sophie stood alone under the mulberry bush where it had all begun. She looked out over the moonlit sea towards the twinkles of Sami in the distance as the water lapped at the pebbly shores that skirted the coast road in front of the restaurant. Clinks from the yacht masts could be heard in the distance and the night bird was again calling for a mate from the pine-clad hillside across the bay. She was instantly thrust back to the very first night she had visited the Sea Rock and had been seated in that very spot. Anna had approached her with her friendly New Zealand accent and made her feel instantly welcome against the insecurities of her lone presence. How different things had been then and how scared she had been about her future. Her mind drifted back to her ex fiancé, James, and how his jilting her at the alter had been the catalyst for her ending up in Kefalonia alone on Honeymoon. If things hadn't happened as they had she would never have met Nikolas, she thought as she looked over at the man that had stolen her heart with his gentle and patient soul. She wondered how different things could have been if things had not happened as they had. She placed her hands on her stomach and looked down at the ever-growing bump.

"This is where it all began. This is where your Papa stole my heart!" she whispered with a smile.

Nikolas watched Sophie as she took a moment under the Mulberry tree. Being sat there alone reminded him of the first time he had seen her face as she had been sat looking lost as he had repaired his fishing nets on Evangeline. Her face had stolen his heart at that very moment. How every night he had a shift at the Sea Rock he had longed to see her looking back at him from that very spot. Now she was sat looking even more beautiful in the moonlight carrying his child and about to become his wife.

He walked over to join her and placed his hands on her stomach.

"I can't wait for us to meet this little gift and for you to become my wife Sophie. Meeting you was the best thing to happen to me after my Maria. I love you more today than I ever thought possible when I first saw your face smiling back at me. You make me so happy every time I look at you," he said as wrapped his arms around her.

Chapter 12

It had taken Amy almost a week to get back in contact with Sophie after she had sent a text message breaking her incredible news. By then, Sophie and Nikolas had already set their ceremony date to the middle of June and Sophie was already fully submersed in Wedding plans.

A familiar ringtone sent Sophie into a rush across the garden in her delicate state to answer a face time call from her oldest friend who was still travelling her way around the world like a womble.

"Can you see me Soph, Can you? I am stuck on this incredibly dull tropical island in the Indian Ocean and the Wi-Fi is a bit crap so I am sorry if I just drop out on you! So anyways, OMFG!! Is the news real, is it really authentic or is it April fools day in Greece! I almost fell off an elephant when I read your message. You're like forty-one now and only just getting life right!! I still haven't even had a chance to vet the father of your child! Let me see!! Stand up so I can see the bump!" Amy said, taking a moment to take a breath.

"Do you know how good it is to see you and hear your voice. Tracking you down is harder than finding life on Mars! I have been desperate to speak to you and tell you the news. You need to get your arse here ready for my Wedding Day as you are Maid of Honour!" Sophie replied, standing up and turning her silhouette sideways so Amy could see her bump.

"Hi baby!! This is Auntie Amy! You can come travel the world with me when you're older. You are going to enjoy your play dates with me. I am so much fun!" she said in the most horrendously squeaky voice.

"Amy it can't hear you! And stop with that voice, its kind of creepy! So anyway, I will text you the date and the details of the Wedding so you can make your way here in whatever fashion you like. As long as you get here on time. You can crash at our Villa or I can find somewhere for you to stay if that suits you better." she said in a rush in case her friend disappeared and they lost signal.

"Whatever! I am cool with anything and you know I wouldn't miss your Wedding. I got to your last one, didn't I! You need me there anyway just in case he does a runner too!" Amy said in jest. "Anyway, I have a massage to get to. Thai massage is so relaxing and I am sure it will help with your pregnancy as you get bigger. Love you and it's so good to see your face. Bye bump, Bye!!" with that, Amy disappeared.

Sophie beamed at her brief conversation with her best friend. She was possibly the most craziest person she knew and managed to live a pretty enviably lifestyle on the very little money she made from writing travel blogs for a living. Amy was the only person who could blag her way around the world for free and always end up in the most amazing locations living the life of the rich and famous on just pennies. Her fierce Eco-chic ways meant Amy needed very little to enjoy life. A good book, a bikini, her backpack and the open road was everything that made her best friend happy. Amy was her rock though no matter how elusive she was. Sophie always knew she had her back and would never let her down.

Texting her the full details of the Wedding, Sophie picked up the telephone and called her Mother who had massaged to tell her that they would be arriving in Kefalonia in a week to spend some extended time with her ahead of the Wedding and to help out where she could.

Planning a Wedding while pregnant had not been easy. Sophie became tired very quickly and the mid-May heat was now starting to make her irritable. The gardens were now a wash with bees that were frantically gathering the pollen from the newly emerging rosemary flowers that surrounded the gardens and sent its welcoming calming scent through the open window's, as Sophie became stressed by the amount of things there were to do.

She was also re-decorating the nursery and making it a neutral space to welcome either a baby boy or girl. They had no desire to find out the sex and had wanted to have the surprise of the reveal after the birth. Sophie planned every detail of the birth down to her birthing clothes and the babies first set of clothes to leave hospital. She wanted everything to be just perfect. Maria visited and brought with her a huge white bunny that sat on the wooden nursing chair in the corner of her once abandoned nursery. She was so excited about becoming a big sister and offered her babysitting services ahead of anyone else.

Cleopatra, her Wedding planner, had come to her aid a few times to calm her stress and taken on a huge role in organising the Wedding as Sophie had no clue where to start. Anna accompanied her to try on a few different Wedding dresses and they had successfully chosen the perfectly pretty flower girl dress for her soon to be niece, Selena. Without any clue when Amy would arrive, Sophie left her to choose her own dress that she insisted she would have made for her while she was in Thailand.

By the end of May, temperatures on Ithaca were now reaching the late twenties and the air was becoming humid making it difficult for her to get a decent night sleep. Nikolas reverted to sleeping on the settee on occasions so he was not too tired leaving the house at 4am to get to his lobster pots. The pool had finally been completed and the gardens were now silent again. Through the day Sophie could now cool off in the serenity of the waters and look out over the chalky blue waters below too calm her hectic mind.

Sophie took a whole day off planning to spend a rare day with Nikolas, so he could show her around the part of Ithaca that she now knew as home. Taking a treacherous narrow dusty road above the neighbouring village of Exhogi, they snaked upwards through the denseness of the cypress trees that swayed seductively above them on either side in the slight morning breeze. Sophie wound down her window, allowing the freshness of the mountain to spill in, igniting her senses with the slightly citrus scents of pine.

Eventually, they came to a stop, parking on a level plateau in front of an old iron gate with thick white pillars topped with white crosses. Sophie stepped out of the car and wandered to a bench that overlooked the entire north side of the island. Looking down, she noted the terraces and clustered terracotta roofs of the charming village of Exhogi perched on the hillside. Her eyes followed the winding road that led into the verdant pine forest to the peacock blue of the coast below. Distant islands erupted from the serenity of the misty horizon, and the endless skyline lay unblemished by any clouds.

Pushing the gate open, they wandered under the shade of an imposing ancient pine tree, momentarily obscuring their open sea vista. As they followed the path of sun-scorched pine needles that had been scattered over the ground for centuries, a pretty whitewashed chapel with a small bell tower sporting a distinctive azure blue roof and doorway, emerged into view. Its simplistic beauty took Sophie by surprise. Trying the handle, she was disappointed to find the door locked. A herd of seemingly tame goats, grazed on any succulents they could find around the bell tower unfazed by their presence.

"It's so peacefully here! Where are we?" she inquired.

"This is the Monastery of Panagia. It is was still being used until after the first world war when Monk Iacovos Mavrokefalos was to renovate the monastery. He had intended to stay here after his retirement. Unfortunately, the Germans executed him during the Second World War. His grave is just over there!" Nikolas replied, pointing towards a small tomb.

"Why would anyone kill a monk?" Sophie said, in disbelief. "I can understand why someone would want to stay here and grow old. The views are so incredible. I don't think there is anywhere on

Ithaca that is so magical." she said, looking over the hypnotising vista towards the north of the neighbouring island of Kefalonia.

"The mountains below Exhogi were almost destroyed by a fierce fire and risked the ancient villages you can see far in the distance. They came with aeroplanes that dropped water from the skies to put out the fires and protect the landscape. Come, we will explore Exhogi next and then maybe take a break. They make the most incredible coffee here in the North of Ithaki," Nikolas suggested and placed his arm around Sophie as he led her back to the car.

As they entered the village, traditional crumbling stone cottages and freshly renovated villa's shared the hillside, all following the steep hill, amphitheatrically overlooking the bay below. Some of the houses were over three hundred years old, with many in ruins from the regular earthquakes and tremors the island endured. Further down the hill and closer to the coast, she could see a cluster of small houses and another church almost lost among the olive and the cypress trees.

Nikolas explained that once sea pirates had been a terrible threat to the Ionian islands and Exhogi had been the main village of the island due to its high position. When the threat of pirates had decreased, lots of the villagers had moved closer to the coast for work and created the other villages that were sparsely spread around the island. They had visited the strange pyramids and pretty church of Agia Marina, with its characteristic blue dome that Sophie could see from their garden that took central pride in the village. They could not explore the church tower as Sophie had hoped due to Earthquake damage. Leaving a donation towards the rebuild of the church, Nikolas took her further into the village, and as Sophie walked past a few of the ancient homes, she noted that they had painted masks, almost human-like, hung by their doorways.

"These are Moros and guard the homes against evil spirits," he explained, noting her lips curl in disgust at these lifelike decorations.

Having taken a coffee break and sharing some halva, they continued their morning adventures. Passing by the sleepy houses of the village, the road continued downwards through the trees and shrubs that coloured the landscape. Reaching the quaint traditional village of Kalamos, Nikolas came to a stop by a bridge. Taking Sophie by the hand, they walked through a dense area of cypresses, olive trees, oaks and strawberry trees until they reached a three-arched building housing a small water fountain.

Sophie took in the serenity of her surroundings as Nikolas explained that this had been where freshwater for King Odysseus palace, that was now in ruins close by, would have been collected by the servants in the royal amphorae, and delivered back to Queen Penelope for her to quench her thirst. A plaque on the wall explained that if the water was drunk, strangers would always return to Ithaca. Turning the tap, Sophie cupped her hands and took a mouthful of the refreshingly cold waters and, for a moment, seemed to be transported back in time. Feeling exhausted by the heat of the day, they headed back to Villa Elysian to take dinner under the shade of the jasmine tree.

It was now early June and Sophie's parents had arrived, a few weeks ahead of the Wedding. Erika had opened her home with welcoming arms to her future English family. She was so happy to have an excuse to bake, cooking up a different traditional meal for her guests every night. Erika seduced Sophie's father with her cooking and humorous character. She hit it off with Sophie's mother almost immediately over their love of bridge, spending so many evenings under the stars playing cards, drinking wine and sharing stories.

Having her parents there gave Sophie another support network. Her mother could not stop fussing over her as her bump had now become so much larger. Arranging a family get together, Nikolas ferried everyone across the Ionian seas, for a meal at the Sea Rock. Taking a seat under the mulberry bush, Sophie's parents were instantly seduced by the views across the bay towards Sami. A jet-black cat wandered across to the table and started to rub itself around everyone's ankles as it wound its way around the table legs. Realising that they had no food to share, the cat turned its nose into the air and made its way towards another table where a couple sat devouring a lamb shank. Sophie's father was mesmerised as he watched the cat work the tables like a professional food prostitute and successfully landed itself a scrap of food from almost everyone who fell for its large sad green eyes.

As she took a mouthful of fresh sea bass, Sophie felt a strange sensation from inside her, almost tickling her stomach.

"Oooo!" she suddenly cried in discomfort and lifting herself from her seat.

"Sophie? What is wrong?" questioned a concerned Nikolas.

"I am not sure. I think I just felt the baby move. It's happening again! It feels so strange!" she said with an unsure smile pulled tightly across her face.

"Does it feel like little butterflies fluttering about inside you?" queried her mother.

"Yes, I guess. It's stopped now." She said, as Nikolas gently placed his hand on her rounded belly.

The moon was full and the stars twinkled overhead as the sound of the ocean played in the background. The surrounding vegetation was filled with Cicades chirping away frantically almost serenading them with their night song. Watching as everyone laughed and chatted over dinner, Sophie smiled to herself as she realised that the baby had first moved about in the very place she had spent so much of her time with Nikolas. This had been the most perfect night with their families.

Sophie and Nikolas took her parents on a few days tour of Kefalonia, taking in a few more sights that Sophie had not previously seen. Hiring a 4 x 4 car, Nikolas followed the windy mountain roads above Sami, dodging a herd of mountain goats that had taken an early morning siesta on the shaded tarmac. As they climbed higher, the coastal village seemed to zoom further and further out of sight, leaving just a hazy smudge of its existence on the horizon.

"The views are incredible," remarked Sophie's Mother, as she spoke for the first time since they had ascended into the mountains.

"Wait until we get to the top. The view here is mind-blowing but the approach is very steep and narrow so please be ready for some scary moments!" replied Nikolas mimicking a small explosion with his fingers against his temple.

Winding down the window, a fresh scent of zesty pine wafted into the car as the shade of the dark fir trees brought a moments relief from the heat of the early summer sun. A herd of small wild horses peacefully grazed as they carefully navigated the narrow pass through the impressive forest of trees. Nikolas took a bumpy track that looked almost in passable but after a few skids and nail biting moments, with Sophie clinging onto
the handle above her head, they eventually came to a stop on a tarmacked area near to a radio mast.

"Thank god that's over! I thought we were going to end up rolling backwards down the mountain. Can we take a different route home Nikolas?" Sophie protested.

As they all got out of the car and collected their picnic, a friendly gentleman with a wide white smile, handed Sophie's father a pamphlet which gave some information about the park.

"Efharisto!" nodded her father as he flicked through the leaflet.

"The walk from here is not to hard, but it might get a little difficult the closer we get to the top. We will take a stop on the way to have

91

a short rest for Sophie as she was too stubborn to stay at home today!" Nikolas scowled, giving Sophie a disapproving stare.

"Nikolas, I am only pregnant and not injured. The mountain air and exercise will do me good, plus how could I not come on this trip today. This is incredible!" she replied as she spun her arms around amplifying the view.

"I will keep an eye on her, don't you worry Nikolas!" Sophie's mother reassured.

Making their way along the dusty track, nothing could be heard apart from the crunching of their footsteps and the occasional bleat of a goat in the distance. A small lizard slinked its way across the dusty path ahead and rushed into a crevice in the rocks.

"Oh Simon!! Its one of those things that we see on the wall in Spain! I didn't know they had them here as well!" Judith exclaimed.

"Of course they do Jude! They are all over the Med,' he responded as Sophie smiled at her parents reaction. They had never really ventured far from home apart from the regular bus holidays to Marbella with the same group of friends they had holidayed with since Sophie had been a child. Her parents had visited almost all of the UK with their weekend coach breaks, yet anything beyond Spain was still very much a mystery.

As they continued their walk, they reached a look out point with a few picnic benches where they took a rest and enjoyed the endless views across the West of the island. The walk had not been to taxing on Sophie and she had enjoyed sharing the beauty of the island with her parents, but as they started to reach the summit, the climb became a little harder and Sophie needed to rest a few times to catch her breathe.

The air was also a little thinner and made her shiver from the unwelcome chill. Popping a cardigan around her shoulders, Sophie reached for Nikolas hand.

"Not much further now, Sophie. The view from the top is sensational and so worth the few hours walk," he said, encouraging her the last few hundred yards.

As they reached the altar at the summit, Sophie felt like she had entered paradise. The clouds seemed to pass underneath her so quickly that she felt as if she was floating. The whole of the island was visible from the peak. Everywhere she looked she could see the ocean below her and all the neighbouring islands. Far to the East she could even make out the mainland of West Greece.

"I am speechless, absolutely speechless," her father said as he stood looking around the panoramic vistas before him.

"I feel so close to the sky up here!" her mother exclaimed.

"This is Megas Soros!" began Nikolas. "It is the highest peak of Mount Ainos and higher than Ben Nevis in the UK! From here you can see all of Kefalonia plus Zakynthos to the South and Lefkada and Ithaca to the North. Just a few metres below us is the ruined temple of Zeus, the Greek God of the sky. The land is very fertile from all the rain we have through winter, so this is also where we grow most of our grapes to make wine. There are many small vineyards scattered across the slopes below!" he smiled. "Also here we have our rare wild horses that are descendants of ancient Greek breeds of the Gods that are now extinct and an extremely rare flower that only grows in these mountains called the Mount Ainos Violet," he continued.

Sophie and her parents were all so taken by the views that they could hardly speak.

"Nikolas, these islands are filled with so much beauty that I don't think I will ever get to see it all in my lifetime!" Sophie eventually said as they made their way back to the car. "These beautiful islands really are the most magical places I have ever visited or, for that, ever lived!"

Chapter 13

The day before the wedding had arrived, and, with no sign of Amy, Anna offered to step in as her substitute, to help a disheartened Sophie get herself dressed. After spending the entire morning trying to get through to Amy on her mobile, Sophie was giving up on her best friend being there at all. Having checked that they had got everything they needed ready for the following morning, Sophie sent Nikolas packing to Erika's house for the evening, allowing her to celebrate her last day of being single with the women.

It was just after midday when her phone burst into life, and a very apologetic Amy was sounding very stressed on the other end of the phone.

"Please don't get mad with me, Soph. Getting a flight here from Thailand is not as easy as I had hoped. I have been in the sky more than on the ground in the past twenty-four hours. They actually have a decent airport here, can you believe! I was expecting a goat shed from how primitive you described the islands! I will be there, I promise. I am just getting in the taxi and heading straight to Sami, like you said. I will let you know when I get to Ithaca. Love you," and with that, she had hung up.

Amy was like a whirlwind. She didn't have time to just chatter away on the phone. She said what was on her mind and disappeared as always. There was no point in trying to call her back as she would be talking the taxi driver to sleep at that moment with her tirade of questions and stories of her travels. She was quite possibly lecturing them over the number of carbon emissions their dated 1990's car was emitting into the atmosphere, forgetting that she had possibly created more atmospheric damage than his car did in a year from the three flights she had taken in the past two days.

But she was here, and that was all that mattered. Making a grovelling call to Nikolas, who had just settled down with Stefano to relax for the afternoon, Sophie pleaded with him to taxi Amy on her arrival from Kefalonia. Sophie never had to plead to much as Nikolas would do anything to make her happy.

It was after 8pm when an exhausted Amy arrived at Villa Elysian. She had just arrived with enough light to see the sunset, turning the limestone cliffs below a dusty orange as it sunk into the horizon.

"Look at you! Look at this! I am just so incredibly happy for you Soph!" Amy said, kissing her belly first before even acknowledging her best friend.

"That Nikolas is a good catch! Thank goodness James dumped you when he did, otherwise, you might never have got to marry such a hunk," she smiled as she gave her best friend a kiss. "Your baby is going to be gorgeous with a mixture of your genes. So, are you going to introduce me?" Amy said, looking around the room at a few unfamiliar faces.

Having introduced Amy to Erika and Anna, they spent the evening catching up, and all took a midnight swim under the stars as they shone brightly in the darkness of the night. The intoxicating fragrance of the wild broom infused with the heady rosemary filled the air with a sweet vanilla perfume and made Sophie feel sleepy. She left everyone drinking on the patio and retired to bed, hoping to get just a few hours of sleep ahead of the morning preparations.

Nikolas had spent the afternoon on the veranda at Philoxenia, waiting patiently for a call from Sophie to pick up her koumbara, Amy. Having checked that he had put the rings safely in his brother's jacket several times, and reading through a small speech that he had written to thank their guests over and over, Nikolas eventually started to relax. A few of his childhood friends had joined him for a few good luck drinks along with Stefano and Sophie's father. Andreas, his oldest friend, had offered to take

Amy to Villa Elysian on his way home, so Nikolas did not break tradition.

Amy eventually arrived at Kioni late evening, and, after a text from Sophie to say that she was waiting by the Spavento Bar, Nikolas and Andreas wandered the road to meet her. Amy was not what Nikolas had expected at all. From everything that Sophie had told him, he had expected quite a large ferocious lady with muscles bigger than his. But Amy was quite the opposite. She was short and slender with long blonde hair that hung tussled to her shoulders and was hidden under a long headscarf tied at the back of her head, just like a gypsy. She had a pretty petite face that was a deep caramel colour and the golden haze of the evening sunset made her look as though she had just stepped out of the pages of a travel magazine. A jewelled nose piercing caught the taverna lights, and her teeth shined white through her infectious smile they were almost luminous in the fading sun.

"Hey. I am Amy. I guess you are Nikolas. Sophie has raved about you for so long that I almost feel I know you quite well," she said, pulling him into a hug and kissing both his cheeks. "And you are?" she said, looking at the attractive man standing next to Nikolas.

"It is a pleasure to meet with you, Amy, I am Andreas, a good friend of Nikolas and I shall be taking you into the mountains to where Sophie is staying. May I get a hug too?" he said, opening his arms to welcome her embrace. "Let me take your bag, and we can head out."

"A ride into the mountains with a dark, handsome stranger, I think my dreams have come true!" she laughed and followed Andreas to his car. Nikolas text Sophie to let her know that Amy was on her way and then headed back to join his small bachelor's party.

Sophie could not sleep. She tossed and turned for most of the night, worrying about the following day. All she could think about was how she had felt when James had jilted her. What would she do if Nikolas changed his mind just like James had? After trying everything from counting sheep to meditating just to get a little bit of shut-eye, Sophie gave up and headed downstairs to make a cup of coffee.

Taking her morning drink onto the patio, she wandered to the Jasmine tree and sat under its shade. She inhaled the heady scent of its morning perfume as the sun rose in the distance. Peach, magenta, amber and rose, radiated across the sky. Watching the colours spill outwards across the rich blue of the sea, it felt as though the warming sun rays were trying to reach out to fill her heart with hope and trust that today would bring the new beginning that she had always yearned for.

Nikolas was up early that morning. He could not sleep with the excitement bubbling away inside him. He poured a mug of coffee and headed out onto the veranda. The morning sunrise was a breath-taking display of radiant colours that slowly overcame the dark blue and purple of the twilight sky. The sun was just peeking out of the horizon, and its brilliant rays already shone brightly and began to warm the air. Nikolas watched the glistening reflection of the sun on the ocean, and a thrilling feeling swept over him as he considered the day ahead. He wondered what Sophie was doing at that very moment and hoped that she realised that he would never let her down.

With everyone at the villa now emerging from their night sleep, it had become a hive of activity and excitement. The hairdresser and makeup artist had arrived and had already set to work transforming a beaming Erika who made everyone giggle with her constant chatter. Breakfast had been a very light affair with a spread of cheeses and pieces of bread accompanied by orange juice. Sophie forced food into herself as her stomach churned with anticipation of the day ahead.

Anna and Amy had both taken it upon themselves to prepare the marital bed, locking Sophie out of the room. They made the bed with freshly made linen, covered it with the traditional flower petals, rice and money ready for the happy couple to return later that evening. The morning seemed to fly by and with everyone else now ready, Amy had a moment alone with Sophie and helped her into her Wedding dress.

Sophie looked so elegant in the flowing white dress she had chosen, and it hung just perfectly over her bump. With a selection of simple white Jasmine flowers from the garden and the soft green of olive branches, her bouquet was stunning. Adding a final touch of bling that Amy had bought as a gift for Sophie in Indian around her wrist, she was ready to slip on her shoes and head to her Wedding ceremony.

"I have never seen you glow with so much happiness Sophie," said her mother as they walked to the car. "I get a feeling that this is going to be the most perfect day for you and the start of all those dreams you have wished for all your life. I cannot begin to tell you how proud of you I am. You look like a perfect Greek Goddess."

The journey to Vathy took them through the mountains and skirted the dramatic coastline seducing Amy with impressive views of the neighbouring island of Kefalonia. The lull of the landscape as it drifted by kept Sophie's mind calm and in no time with the singing and constant chattering of the group, they had arrived at Vathy Harbour.

As she stepped out of the bridal car, she was greeted with shouts and claps from the occupants of the many surrounding taverna's. Tears fell from her fathers face as he saw how beautiful Sophie looked as she walked towards him in the warm Ithacan sunshine. Proudly taking his daughters arm, they walked to an awaiting boat that had been decorated in pretty white ribbons and bunting. Taking the Bridal party for the short ride to Lazaretto island, the captain returned for Sophie and her father. Musicians accompanied them playing bouzouki love songs as they made the journey across the water to the chapel. Honking his horn, the captain announced the arrival of the bride as Sophie and her father stepped off the boat to be welcomed by the sound of the church bells ringing her arrival across the bay. That simple moment with her father had been incredibly emotional and Sophie had felt like royalty with the attention her arrival had caused.

Now they were at the chapel, Sophie felt so nervous. Taking a deep breath, she followed the line of decorated bay trees that defined the outdoor aisle. She anxiously waited under the shaded canopy of trees that had been decorated with swathes of bunting that flapped in the gentle sea breeze. She caught a glimmer of Nikolas waiting eagerly for her arrival, and she felt herself relax. He was there. This was actually happening. She was about to get married. As the music began to play, Nikolas turned, and a smile spread across his face as his beautiful bride smiled back at him. Tears of joy ran uncontrollably down Sophie's face, sending her mascara running down her cheeks like an iconic 1980s rock star. Taking a moment to wipe her eyes, Sophie made her way down the aisle.

Chapter 14

The days after the Wedding seemed to drift by in a hazy pink mist as Sophie settled into her new role as Mrs. Manolatos. They had spent a few romantic days alone together at Villa Elysian before embarking on a surprise honeymoon that Nikolas had arranged for his new wife. Amy had also surprised Sophie and remained on Ithaca having been seduced by the serenity of the island and by Nikolas' friend, Andreas after many shots of Mastiha. They had both instantly hit it off as Andreas ran the spiritual retreat in the mountains on the west side of Ithaca that Nikolas had once pointed out from Evangeline. In fact, Sophie had only had a few texts from her best friend as she explained that she and Andreas had been very busy experimenting with different intimate Yoga poses.

Having packed just a small bag of essentials, Nikolas and Sophie had travelled across to Agia Efimia on-board Evangeline to start their honeymoon. Sophie had no clue where they were going and had expected to be travelling to the airport. Instead, Nikolas had escorted her just a short walk along the harbour to a beautiful white sailing yacht that was bobbing about on the water.

"This is our home for the next few days, Sophie. I will be your captain for the journey, and we shall be visiting all around the Ionian seas, like pirates" he said, making a low bow.

"This is just perfect, Nikolas. I can't wait to set sail!" she replied excitedly stepping on board.

Taking her small overnight bag below deck, Sophie marvelled at the cosiness of their cabin. She had never been inside a yacht before. Everything was fitted in a wooden style finish and so compact but with absolutely everything that they needed for a comfortable stay.

With the tour of their accommodation taking only a few minutes, Sophie re-joined Nikolas up on deck. Sophie had no clue what she was supposed to do and waited for some instructions from Nikolas who was already rigging the boat ready to set sail.

Having spent a few moments going over the basics of sailing with Sophie and kitting her out with a life jacket just in case she was toppled overboard, Nikolas started up the motor and having lifted the anchor, they set out for open waters.

Being on the yacht was so different to Nikolas smaller fishing boat. It seemed to glide through the water effortlessly as they made their way towards the peninsular next to Sami. Sophie had never explored the southern part of Kefalonia and was excited by their upcoming adventures. She was also glad that they were not travelling far as she was almost seven months pregnant and her bump tired her out so quickly. Staying close to Kefalonia was reassuring.

As they reached the open waters, Sophie took hold of the helm as Nikolas quickly eased out the sail and secured the lines as they made their way up wind. Taking back control of the helm from a panicking Sophie, Nikolas handled the boat so naturally. He zig zagged it back and forth, tacking into the wind so it captured the sail making the boat tip gently from side to side and propelling it forward.

Sophie watched as the lush landscape drifted by. The dazzling white beach of Antisammos, made infamous by the film Captain Corelli's Mandolin and actors, Penelope Cruz and Nichols Cage, looked like a hidden paradise from the sea. The dense green rolling hills and lush vegetation intensified the hues of the translucent turquoise waters that lapped at the pure white pebbly shore. The rows of perfectly positioned sunbeds and umbrellas were enough to entice any passing sailing boats to drop anchor and spend a few delicious hours soaking up the warm rays of sunshine on this mesmerizing beach.

As Antisammos bay drifted from view, they followed the island south hugging the coastline. The endless vistas of majestic olive green mountains that stretched to the edge of the sea leaving just a small exposed rocky white limestone belt before the land plunged into the blue beneath. Untouched by any kind of development, nature had effortlessly created a tranquil beauty that had Sophie hypnotised for hours. The occasional seabird flew out from the density of the tree canopies, echoing its cries across the water and diving into the depths to emerge with a fish flapping about in its beak. The wildness of this spectacular landscape could only experienced from the sea as no roads carved through the treeline or ascended from the hilltops above.

In the distance, a picturesque village settled into the base of the surrounding hills came into view. This had been the first sighting of human life that Sophie had encountered on the entire journey from Antisammos beach. As they sailed by Sophie noted how sleepy the village had looked. Just a few yachts were moored in one of the two ports and a scattering of people wandered the harbour side and bathed on its narrow pebbly beach.

"This is Poros," advised Nikolas. "It was once a trendy holiday destination many years ago, the very first place for tourists to stay on all of Kefalonia. The ferries from the mainland still dock here but time seems to have forgotten this ancient village," Nikolas said. "Those giant rocks close to the beach were said to have been thrown at Jason and the Argonauts and many pirates by the Cyclopes who protected our island," he continued, pointing to the shore.

The history of this island and strong beliefs in its ancient mythology ignited the adventurer in Sophie and, with every little morsel of knowledge she absorbed from Nikolas, the more she was captivated. Continuing their voyage, Nikolas suggested taking a stop for a much-needed cool off from the intense June sunshine.

As they followed the south coast of the island, Nikolas explained that as the island was on a seismic fault line, with every earthquake a new beach or cove emerged from the seas. This meant that there were now so many secret coves that no one had ever stepped foot. The island really was magical, he smiled as he dropped the anchor in the prettiest secluded bay that Sophie had seen. Large grey and peach boulder like cliffs, topped with a blanket of lush green vegetation, jutted out like cannons over the turquoise sea. Naturally formed caves exposed a few smaller bays beyond and provided a natural shade from the heat of the sun.

"This is Kato Lagadi beach! We shall take a swim and cool off in the water," Nikolas announced, as he stripped down to his swim trunks and dived off the boat into the .

The water looked so calm and inviting that Sophie did not need any convincing. Proudly revealing her perfectly rounded bump in her maternity swim costume, she joined Nikolas in the clear refreshing salt waters below. Spending a while chasing the shoals of multi-coloured fish that fed from the colourful corals on the seabed and wandering through the caves that joined each bay, they enjoyed the isolation of the cove to themselves almost all morning before heading back on board and continuing on their sleepy voyage.

Just a little further along the coast, an endless expanse of sand came into view filled with holidaymakers soaking up the sun and backed by a dramatic pine-forest. From the amount of hotels, tavernas and apartments that dotted the landscape, it appeared to be a bustling resort. As they approached, Sophie noted how much livelier this part of the island was in contrast to the other places they had visited.

Drifting past, Nikolas advised that they had just passed Skala and would be docking in neighbouring port of Katelios for the evening. Reaching a small marina that jutted out from the bottom of a steep hill, Sophie took in the relaxing surroundings of this small fishing village as Nikolas busied himself preparing to dock. Sophie did her best to help under Nikolas instructions and after successfully lowering the sail, she felt very accomplished.

Having tied the mooring ropes securely, Sophie followed Nikolas to one of the tavernas along the pebbly seafront where they sat drinking on a cold Mythos while watching a few local children playing in the water in front of them. The day had almost disappeared and Sophie was now extremely hungry from being so submersed by the calming sea air. Ordering a recommended fish dinner, they sat and enjoyed the laid back atmosphere. The fertile fields beyond yielded a scattering of private villas that served the handful of sleepy taverna's along the beach. This was the traditional side of Kefalonia that Sophie liked most. Long gone were the days of wanting to be surrounded by hoards of people or partying the night away. Now she was content watching the sunset over a nice traditional meal in a quiet taverna and, after filling her stomach, retiring to an early bed feeling contented.

They had spent the time over their evening meal discussing the history of the surrounding islands and those he had visited during the time he had spent on the Ionian seas with his Papa. How his Papa had taught him to hold his breath for a long time and hunt for fish in the depths around the coast in the traditional ways using only a spear gun. Having filled their hunger with the most delicious grilled fish whilst being serenaded by the sounds of the cicadas that filled the night, Sophie needed her bed.

Chapter 15

Nikolas was up early the next morning with the sunrise preparing breakfast for Sophie who had had the best night sleep in such a long time. Eventually Sophie emerged from below deck, joining a cheery Nikolas who had laid the most perfect spread of Erika's home baked bread and cheese. She had joined him in enough time to capture the colourful display on the horizon before the sun finally rose in the sky. Nikolas was so excited about the day ahead as he had planned to take her far out in the Ionian seas away from Kefalonia, to a little known island that he had last visited as a boy. Sophie was unsure how she felt about being so far from land but trusted her husbands knowledge of the seas to keep them safe.

Setting sail from Katelios, Sophie nervously watched Kefalonia gradually disappear behind them. Nikolas pointed the yacht into the void ahead and sailed out into the open seas. The ocean was so much choppier and the stronger wind picked up the sail sending them at quite a speed across the crests of the waves. Sophie attached her safety line to the surrounding rail as she felt the boat lean sideways into the water and had her holding on for dear life to stop her disappearing into the depths below.

Being so far from shore and not seeing another vessel anywhere on the horizon was the most vulnerable that Sophie had ever felt in her entire life. She felt so small against the depths and vastness of the ocean ahead of her. She noted a large landmass on the horizon that Nikolas advised was Zakynthos, another of the Ionian islands. The island he was taking her to lay further south in complete remoteness and would be at least another hour at sea.

A shoal of dolphins joined them for part of the journey, playfully jumping in the wake of the boat and breaching the waters ahead of them. These magical creatures kept Sophie entertained and her mind off the depths of the sea below them. After a while, Sophie noted a tiny island emerge from the distant waters and pointed its appearance to Nikolas. This had been the first sighting of land that Sophie had seen in a considerable amount of time and its presence had been welcoming.

"That is where we are heading Sophie. The unknown Ionian islands of Strofades. This is where I believe my Papa went missing. This is where his flare was seen and his last distress call had been received," Nikolas explained.

The closer to the islands the sailing boat came, the more Sophie could see how he might have been caught on the rocks. Two small islands sat side by side separated by just a shallow rocky plateau with a turbulence of sea stopping any craft from sailing between. The smallest of the islands was barren and flat with no place to land a boat yet the larger of the islands was fascinating. A single imposing building sat eerily neglected against the waters edge. Huge metals rods that made it look as though it was on the verge of collapse held its castle like stone tower together. A small landing jetty jutted out from the undergrowth. The island had now obvious signs of life apart from the birds filled the skies above. Nature had claimed the island for itself.

"What is this place?" she questioned looking at Nikolas who had dropped anchor a safe distance from the rocky shore.

Joining Sophie on the deck Nikolas explained from the memory of what he had been told as a young lad.

"These are the uninhabited islands of the Strofades, once said to be the hiding place of one of the Harpies, Aeollo, whom was pursued by Jason and the Argonauts before he headed to the temple of Zeus on Mount Ainos in Kefalonia. It was later said to be cursed and for centuries inhabited by just pirates. These islands are so remote that their existence is not even known to most Greeks," he remarked.

"This is the bigger of the two islands, Stamafi. The crumbling hulk you see was an important monastery, built centuries ago, under the orders of Princess Penelope, daughter of an emperor, who was saved by these islands from a shipwreck. A large community of monks lived a harsh life here for centuries, farming the land and fishing the seas to survive. This building once hid an earthly paradise filled with treasures. The pirates would kill the monks or take them for slaves to trade after raiding their treasures. This is where Saint Dionysus studied before he became the protector of Zakynthos. After his death he was returned here to be buried but his remains had to be moved to stop them being stolen by sea pirates. After many earthquakes, the monastery became fragile and many of the monks left or passed away on the island," he said taking a breath.

"Eventually just one monk, Father Gregory Kladis, remained on the island with only the company of the lighthouse keeper and his wife. That was until they modernised the lighthouse and they no longer needed anyone to look after the lights. Then, the monk remained completely alone on the island, visited once a month by a boat that had been sent with provisions from neighbouring monasteries. He stayed for almost thirty years with only the company of nature, trying to maintain the monastery from falling into disrepair, until his health deteriorated and he was taken to hospital on Zakynthos. He never returned. He was eighty when he passed away. His story is known by just a few as the last Monk of Strofades. For many years the island has been left abandoned and lays forgotten. Left to nature and the birds to enjoy. The orchards are filled with the once tendered fruits that now go to waste. The monastery is now silent and filled with the ghosts of its past. People tried to raise monies for the monastary to be made safe for visitors to enjoy but this takes time and if there is no help soon, this will soon fall into the seas. If it is lost it will never be rebuilt," he finished.

"That's a sad story. I can't imagine how anyone could spend thirty years alone on an island. That is a long time. So this whole island is now deserted and no one lives there at all?" Sophie enquired.

"No one is allowed to step foot on this island as it is protected for marine life only. I have always wanted to wander the monastery and visit in the gardens in hope that my Papa had found his way to safety but we can be put in prison for this," he shrugged. "It was something that gave me hope that he might still be alive, but I know that this is not the case."

Sophie looked at the sad building that yearned to be remembered and hoped that the money would be raised to bring this piece of history back to life before the oceans swallowed it for good.

They spent the remainder of the day visiting along the golden sands of Kalamaki on Zakynthos, Sophie had watched in complete awe as the sandy beach had filled with the activity of freshly hatched baby loggerhead turtles, frantically racing along the sands, driven by their natural instincts towards the calm safety of the surf. They had travelled to the north of the island and moored in the turquoise waters just off the coast of the sheltered Navagio cove with its iconic shipwreck, where they stayed overnight. Waking up to the dramatic sheer white limestone cliffs, contrasting blue hues of the sky and seas, the lush green vegetation that outlined the landscape and the vibrant oranges of the salt rusted metal skeleton that lay grounded on the perfect white pebbly beach, Sophie felt she had woken on the set of Pirates of the Caribbean, and half expected Johnny Depp to stagger drunkenly across the deserted sands.

After an incredible few days, they made their way back towards Kefalonia. It had been a fine morning and the fresh north-westerly winds had given perfect conditions for a great morning of sailing. Taking advantage of the consistent breeze, Nikolas had steered the boat further from the coast so they could glide in the calm seas and enjoy their last few hours on board. After a few hours of carving through the incredible blues of the open seas, the wind suddenly picked up. Nikolas noted dark clouds looming on the horizon and feared an unexpected storm approaching. The sky above became darker the further north they travelled. Eventually the storm clouds had completely blacked out the sun and the air had become uncomfortably humid. The heavens opened as a tirade of rain emptied onto the deck and a bolt of lightening lit up the clouds above. Nikolas instructed Sophie to align the boom with the wind direction, raise the main sail to its fullest, tighten up the jib sail and make sure all the ropes were secured as he battled against the strengthening winds and surging waves to keep the boat on course. He checked the wind speed from the sensor on the top of the mast and noted that the wind was ranging near gale force.

Sophie had never been so scared. She had no clue what she was doing even though Nikolas had been over the process a few times during the days they had been aboard. She secured her safety line to the side of the boat and held onto the mast for dear life as she did what she had been told then tightened the reef line making sure it was locked in place. The deck was slippery with the wetness of the rain and the movement of the boat made it even more difficult for Sophie. The yacht suddenly thrust forward as she opened the main sail and it caught the strong wind. Sophie was momentarily lifted into the air as a large wave sent the front of the boat suddenly downwards causing it to break on the deck. As she frantically tried to secure the ropes, the boom became loose and caught her bump as it sped passed her. Sophie winced in pain as she managed to catch her breath and secure the heavy boom in position.

Nikolas held onto the helm with all his strength as he watched helplessly as Sophie battled with the ropes. He was desperate to send her to the safety of the deck below until after the storm had passed. There would be no way that he could keep the boat afloat with out her help during the raging of the sudden summer squall. The waves were now lapping the deck and he knew that they could hit his precious Sophie into the depths with the force of their impact. All he could think about was their unborn child and how he had promised to keep her safe. He noted the boom strike Sophie as it cam unleashed and her hold her stomach from the unexpected impact.

With the ropes all tightened and now secured, an exhausted Sophie retreated to the safety of the deck below. Unbearable pains shot through her abdomen as she tried to breath through the discomfort. As Nikolas continued to battle with the storm, Sophie paced the small area of the galley. The pains had not eased and seemed to be intensifying. She made her way into the bathroom as she felt a warm wetness below. Pulling down her underwear she noted a small amount of blood. Sophie panicked. She didn't know what to do. They were miles away from land and she needed to know that the baby was OK.

Suddenly, without any warning she felt a gush of warm wetness from below. The pain returned and had intensified. Sophie knew exactly what was happening. Her waters had broken and she was in labour. She screamed for Nikolas who could not hear her over the winds above deck. Sophie was alone, scared and wanted her husband by her side.

After an hour of battling the winds and keeping the boat on course, Nikolas was exhausted. The storm had taken them both by surprise but he was so proud of his wife for securing the sails as quickly as she had with her little knowledge of sailing. Her actions had stopped the boat from tipping with the sudden surge of the waves and disappearing into the darkness below. He was still concerned about the impact he had witnessed and was desperate to get below deck to check on Sophie. After the wind had subsided and the waters had retained their calmed appearance, Nikolas rushed into the cabin.

"Sophie! What's happened?" he said looking at his wife who was doubled over on the floor, completely naked from the waist down.

"The baby is coming Nikolas. I can feel it. It's too early yet. I have another two months to go at least. We need to get to help. I need to get to the hospital!!" she cried in urgency.

"It is another few hours sail from here. I am not sure we will make it in enough time Sophie. I cannot believe how stupid I have been to put you in danger." He said, holding his head in his hands.

Sophie felt another pain shoot through her body as she had a sudden urge to push.

"I can't wait hour's Nikolas. You will have to help me deliver our baby!" she said, fighting against her natural instincts.

In no time the contractions were just minutes apart and Sophie could barely speak from the pain that she was experiencing. Sophie felt sick from the pain. Her body felt as if it was being ripped apart and there was little break between contractions. She started to claw at her clothes and managed to get herself undressed as the urge to push became too intense to ignore. Her body had started to tire but with Nikolas calming words of encouragement she allowed her body to take control.

Another contractions passed and with a strong feeling of needing the toilet Sophie felt the head of the baby emerge. Nikolas had just enough time to check around its neck and with one last push their daughter arrived into the world.

"Sophie, we have a daughter!" he exclaimed with sheer elation of the moment. The he sat backwards in silence not believing what had just happened.

Nikolas was rendered speechless. He had actually delivered his own daughter. He grabbed a towel from the cupboard and wrapped her in the warm softness. She was tiny but perfect in everyway.

"Why isn't she crying Nikolas, What's wrong. Is everything OK? Don't let anything happen to our baby!" she cried in desperation.

Nikolas panicked. He had not even noticed she had not been breathing. He had no idea what he should do. He rubbed the limp body of the tiny human being he held in his hands and hoped that the movement would stimulate a response, just as he had done with the lifeless street kittens he had brought back from the brink of death as a child.

"Come on! Breath! Please breath! I will not let you go not you too!"
he said in complete panic, as he rubbed his daughters tiny chest
and flashed back to the moment he had lost his Evangeline.

Sophie watched helplessly as her body continued to painfully
contract , eventually pushing out the placenta.

After what felt like the longest few minutes, a sudden cry erupted
from the small bundle between Nikolas arms. Her small body
filled with life as a rosy glow covered her peachy skin.

"You did it Sophie! My beautiful Sophie. Meet our daughter!"
Nikolas said lowering the tiny bundle onto her chest and beaming
with pride.

Sophie was exhausted and relieved. She had never experienced so
much pain in all her life, but as she looked into her daughter's
eyes, everything suddenly disappeared. To feel there daughter's
naked skin against her's, sent her emotions on fire with a love that
she had never felt before. She gently kissed her daughter and
breathed in the scent that would bond them for life. Her perfect
tiny fingers spread wide as they searched the air and gripped
firmly onto Sophie's little finger. A dark fuzz of hair covered her
petite head and her skin glowed a warm rosy pink. Sophie looked
at Nikolas who was sat next to her on the galley floor. Happiness
flooded from his eyes as he looked at his amazing wife and their
perfect daughter.

"Rosemary, I would like to name her Rosemary!" said Sophie with
a smile.

Nikolas lent forward, kissed Sophie tenderly on her forehead and
pulled her into his chest. In that moment, his emotions had been
taken on the most incredibly exhausting journey, having
experienced both fear and love. Fear of losing their daughter and
the deepest love and respect he felt for Sophie. He knew nothing
in the world was more precious than what he held between his

arms. His eyes absorbed the beauty of the moment and a rush of the purest love filled his heart. Pushing himself up off the floor, he climbed the stairs to the upper deck and breathed in the calmness of the aftermath of the storm he had just battled. A storm that could have taken this moment of happiness away. Taking the helm, he pointed the boat in the direction of home. He could not wait to get them both back to the safety of Villa Elysian, sit beneath the shade of the jasmine tree and watch as their very own Rosemary grew.

Printed in Great Britain
by Amazon